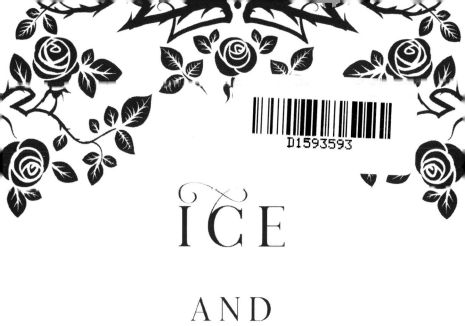

ICE

AND

EMBERS

STEAMPUNK SNOW QUEEN

MELANIE KARSAK

Ice and Embers

Clockpunk Press, 2017

Published by Clockpunk Press.

This work includes lines adapted from
William Shakespeare's *A Midsummer Night's Dream.*

Book design by *Inkstain Design Studio*
Cover design by *Karri Klawiter*
Edited by *Becky Stephens Editing*
Proofread by *Rare Bird Editing*

for Becky

THIS BOOK BELONGS TO:

_____

ICE

AND

EMBERS

LONDON, 1814

The River Thames Frost Fair Handbill

Behold, the frozen Thames

River transformed into an icy wonderland

Come one and all to taste her delights

Under the faerie globes and starry nights

O'er the banks, rejoice in frozen sweets

From beef to cream to bawdy treats

Tamesis calls London's children

To her mirrored surface frozen o'er again

Where winter's kiss trapped faerie revels in her cold embrace

And where man and fish drink as if in a race

Upon the surface of the Thames, gather 'round

Here, where Frostiana will be crowned

You who come here are destined to tell

Of what upon a midwinter night befell

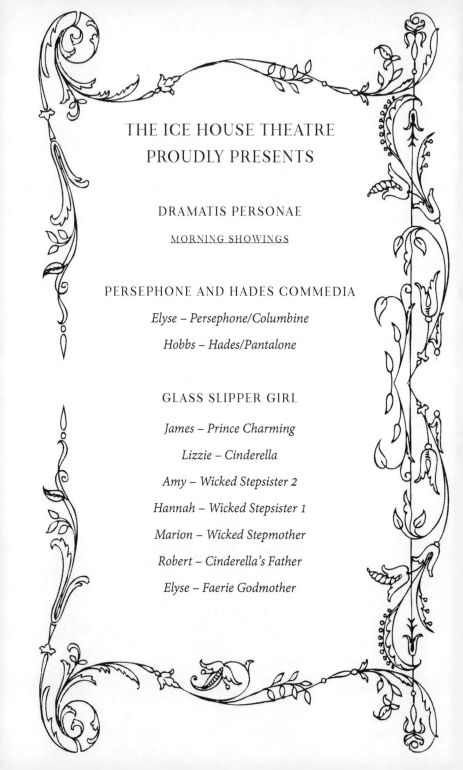

THE ICE HOUSE THEATRE
PROUDLY PRESENTS

DRAMATIS PERSONAE
MORNING SHOWINGS

PERSEPHONE AND HADES COMMEDIA

Elyse – Persephone/Columbine

Hobbs – Hades/Pantalone

GLASS SLIPPER GIRL

James – Prince Charming

Lizzie – Cinderella

Amy – Wicked Stepsister 2

Hannah – Wicked Stepsister 1

Marion – Wicked Stepmother

Robert – Cinderella's Father

Elyse – Faerie Godmother

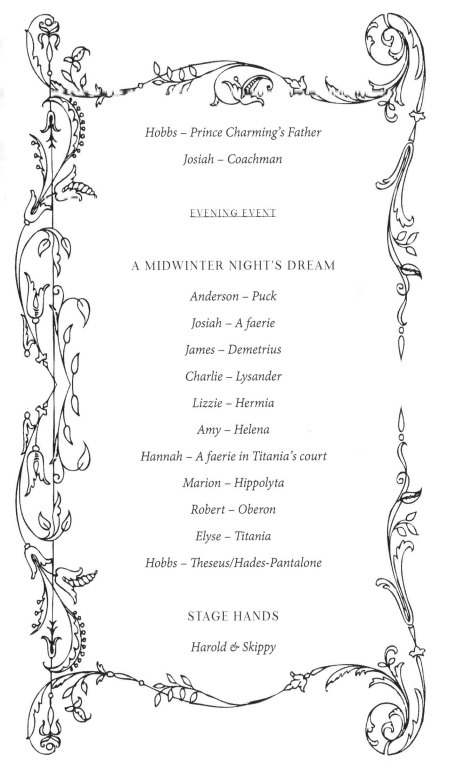

Hobbs – Prince Charming's Father

Josiah – Coachman

A MIDWINTER NIGHT'S DREAM

Anderson – Puck

Josiah – A faerie

James – Demetrius

Charlie – Lysander

Lizzie – Hermia

Amy – Helena

Hannah – A faerie in Titania's court

Marion – Hippolyta

Robert – Oberon

Elyse – Titania

Hobbs – Theseus/Hades-Pantalone

STAGE HANDS

Harold & Skippy

1

A MIDWINTER NIGHT'S DREAM

I EXHALED DEEPLY. MY BREATH, heated by the passion of the kiss, slipped from between my lips and turned into a hazy cloud in the freezing winter air.

"Elyse," John whispered, taking the pale blonde hair at the back of my neck into a gentle handful. He pulled me toward him again. His other hand, located on my lower back, gently pressed my hips toward his. I fell into the crush of his body and felt his warmth and want. I didn't pull away. This was everything I'd ever dreamed of. The idea that a man of his station could fall in love with a girl *like me* was impossible. But still, here I was.

"Elyse, five minutes," Marve, the manager of our acting troupe, shouted. When he spotted us, however, a blush crept up on his cheeks, and he disappeared backstage once more.

"I believe you're needed, Titania," John said. He stepped back and looked me over then straightened the collar on my costume. "Your makeup will need to be touched up. I'm afraid I smeared it a bit."

"I need to start carrying a hand mirror," I said with a soft smile.

"Lovely faerie queen," John whispered in my ear, pausing to kiss my earlobe. "Don't let Oberon have the better of you."

"Never. Are you staying to watch?"

He nodded. "Wouldn't miss it for the world."

I reached out to touch his face. The cold air had made the hollows of his cheeks red. "There are braziers near the front benches where your peers will be sitting. You'll be warm there."

He gently took my hand and kissed my wrist. He stroked his finger across the blue veins below my pale skin. Lifting his eyebrows in a mischievous arch, he asked, "Do you think there is anywhere on this frozen river that's warm?"

"In my arms?" I replied, mirroring his playful expression.

He laughed. "That's the best, and most correct, answer."

I grinned playfully. "If you wanted to be warm, then coming to the Frost Fair was a wretched idea."

"But if I hadn't come, I wouldn't have seen my faerie queen."

I smiled and looked deeply into his honey-colored eyes. My heart beat so hard I felt like it was going to burst. If I wasn't careful, my passion for

John was going to make me swoon. Kai would say I was being ridiculous, that swooning was a fashion, not a physical malady.

At the front of the theatre, I heard the sounds of flutes and horns. The play was starting.

Marve appeared once more. Too stressed to remain courteous, he huffed at me. "Elyse…Lord Waldegrave, I'm sorry, but we really do need our faerie queen."

"I need to go," I whispered.

"My apologies," John called to Marve then turned to me. "See you soon, Titania," he said, kissing the back of my hand. He then turned and headed toward the front of the house, such as it was, situated on the frozen Thames.

I sighed heavily, gathered up the long skirts of my costume, and headed for the stairs.

Forgetting myself, my head lost in love, I nearly slipped on the ice.

"Fool," I cursed myself, giggling. I steadied myself against the side of the makeshift theatre. When I reached the top of the steps, I paused and looked out at the ice. For the first time in many years, the Thames had frozen solid. The Frost Fair had popped up on the ice practically overnight. Thus far, our company from the Struthers Theatre, which we'd renamed the Ice House Theatre in homage to our temporary venue, was the only one to take advantage of the limited opportunity. I looked out across the frozen Thames. Glimmering hues of amber, pomegranate red, and deep purple streaked the sky as the sun dipped below the horizon.

The colors cast an opalescent hue on the frozen river.

I exhaled happily. I had fallen in love with a fine gentleman and he with me. Our amour was not without complications, but it wasn't uncommon for a man of good station to fall in love with an actress. Other lords had taken singers or ladies of the stage as wives. Our relationship would need to be discreet until he got his family's approval. I wouldn't want to sully his reputation in any way. But I was a skilled ballerina and actress, had good manners, and was attractive. That counted for something, didn't it? Even if I didn't have good breeding, that didn't mean I couldn't become Lady Waldegrave.

"Elyse," Marve whispered, his voice a sharp hiss. Master Shakespeare called. I smiled, wondering what the Bard would think of our frozen rendition of his work, which we'd playfully titled *A Midwinter Night's Dream*.

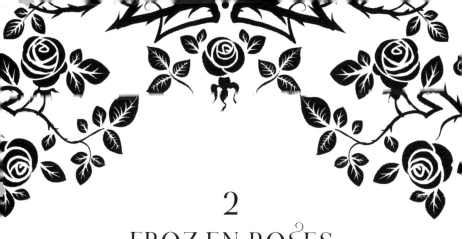

2
FROZEN ROSES

AS I STOOD STAGE LEFT, my eyes closed, I listened to the banter of Anderson, who played Puck, and Josiah, who played a faerie. I laced my fingers together and breathed in the frozen air. I made myself into Titania. My husband—well, Titania's husband—whom I'd once loved deeply, would stop at nothing to hurt me. From his many affairs to his ridiculous request that I give him the orphaned boy I watched over, he always sought to pain me. I loved my husband, and I hated him.

I felt tears—Titania's tears—well up in my eyes.

"And here is my mistress," Josiah called, cueing Oberon's and Titania's entrance on stage.

I opened my eyes and nodded to Hannah, who was dressed as a faerie. She held the train of my dress. She wore a blue and white dress and silver wings to appear the part of a frost faerie. I took a deep breath and stepped on stage.

The Ice House Theatre had been hastily constructed. There was a small, wooden stage that stood just a few feet above the audience and supporting beams for a curtain. Rows of rough cut timber benches sat before the stage. Braziers burned brightly, illuminating the crowd and warming the attendees. Behind the benches was standing room. Tenting had been used to enclose the space save the entryway, through which I had a view of the Frost Fair outside. I looked out at the festivities. My eyes skimmed the scene. On the frozen Thames, a small city of tents had been erected practically overnight. Intermixed with the makeshift stalls were ships trapped in the frozen river. I heard rowdy voices coming from the temporary taverns, smelled the scent of roasted pecans on the bitterly cold breeze, and caught a glimpse of the masts of ships frozen in their ports. Revelers ice-skated down Freezeland Lane just outside the theatre. The Frost Fair was in full swing.

The sound of applause pulled me back. The crowd stretched all the way to the entrance. Several members of the gentry sat on the benches at the front. Behind them stood the commoners.

"Ill met by moonlight, proud Titania," Robert, who played Oberon, called to me from across the stage.

I let Elyse disappear and summoned Titania once more. All at once, I was overwhelmed by Titania's confused feelings of love and anger. I clenched my jaw and fought back Titania's tears, my heart beating quickly as Titania wondered how her husband could so willingly hurt her.

"What, jealous Oberon?" I retorted, smiling sardonically at him. Titania's bitter words were a mask for the pain her heart felt.

Oberon glared at me. "Rash woman. Aren't I your lord?"

"Then I must be your lady. But are you my lord? That didn't seem to concern you when you left Faerieland to take the guise of Corin to make love to Phillida," I retorted angrily as I crossed the stage.

I eyed the benches. Where had John gone? I didn't see him amongst the fine company gathered there. Perhaps he was too late to take a seat amongst his peers.

I turned once more to Oberon. "And now you've come from the farthest reaches of India to see your favorite lover, the bouncing Amazon Hippolyta, be forced to wed Theseus. Your buckskinned mistress, your warrior love. What, have you come to bless her womb one last time before Theseus fills your place?"

The crowd snickered at the subtle bawdy joke. I scanned the crowd once more. John wasn't there. But at the back of the crowd, leaning against a tall pole, was Kai. My lips twitched into a smile at the sight of my forever-friend. His dark hair was tousled in the wind, an ever-present scowl on his face. He may have looked like he was sour, but I knew better. He was concentrating. And at that moment, he was concentrating on me.

When he noticed me looking at him, his gaze softened. His arms were folded across his chest, but he lifted his fingers in the slightest of acknowledgments so not to distract me from my work. It was the same signal he'd used since the first time I took the stage, letting me know he was there and watching. That little move made the knot in my stomach uncurl, and suddenly I felt more relaxed.

"Shame on you, Titania. You, who love Theseus so well that you've led him from woman to woman, from Perigenia to Aegles to Ariadne to Antiopa, breaking hearts in your wake. For what?" Oberon spat at me. "Are you jealous of Hippolyta?"

I looked away from Kai and let Titania fill my mind once more, her thoughts becoming mine.

Fury in my eyes, I turned on Oberon. "Don't pretend you are jealous of the attention I paid to Theseus," I began, then was lost to Titania's words.

Exchanging barbs with Oberon, I let *my* thoughts take second place to Titania. And before I knew it, my scene was done. In a huff, Titania turned and left the stage.

Behind me, the crowd broke out into raucous applause.

Smiling widely, Charlie and Lizzie, who played Hermia and Lysander, stood just off stage.

"Amazing, Elyse," Lizzie whispered.

"Elyse who? I see only Titania," Charlie said, clapping me on the shoulder.

"Was it all right?" I whispered to Lizzie.

"You jest! You *were* Titania," she replied.

"Marvelous, Elyse," Marve whispered, joining us. "We never get applause mid-scene. I teared up at the end when you spoke of the orphaned boy," he said as he adjusted my gown.

Through a very slight crack in the wood of the makeshift backstage, I peered out at the crowd. I still didn't see John.

"Now, when you lie down to sleep in Titania's bower in your next scene, be sure your sleeping face is still visible to the audience. Be the picture of an angel. Like this," Marve said, folding his hands together and pressing them against his cheek. He smiled serenely, but the angelic expression looked very odd on his bearded face, his bushy eyebrows arching sweetly.

I giggled. "Of course. Did you happen to see Lord Waldegrave in the audience?"

"I...I don't know. Elyse, are you listening to me? An angel, do you hear me?"

"Yes, of course, a sleeping angel. I thought he was going to join the gentlemen at the front, but I don't see him there. Did you notice him in the crowd?"

"Actresses," Marve said with a huff. "It's no wonder they used only male actors in Master Shakespeare's day." He rolled his eyes playfully then turned to help the others. "Angel, got it?"

I smiled. "Yes. Indeed. Halo and all."

At that, Marve smiled then went off to coach Lizzie.

FOR THE NEXT TWO HOURS, I played the part of Titania. I tried to ignore my worries about John, but they kept popping up nonetheless. Where had he gone? Thankfully, Kai stayed fixed in his spot. His little nods of reassurance kept me focused. As the play progressed, Titania fought more with Oberon, fell in love with Bottom, who was wearing a donkey's head, and slept facing the crowd looking like an angel. Before I knew it, I reached my final scene.

Reconciled by the end of the play, Titania and Oberon wove around the lovers who lay sleeping on the stage: Theseus with Hippolyta, Helena with Demetrius, and Lysander with Hermia.

"Hand in hand, with faerie grace, we will sing and bless this place," I said, smiling down at the sleeping pairs. Then I twirled around the couples. My soft pink ballet slippers made me feel light on my feet. Calling upon my training as a ballerina, I pirouetted around the pairs, sprinkling a mixture of flowers and silver-colored flecks of paper onto the couples as I moved, blessing their union. The shiny paper glimmered like faerie dust in the shadowed stage light.

As I wove, I glanced at the crowd, feeling the love they had for the illusion I'd created. They didn't see an actress, they saw Titania, the Faerie Queen, blessing the lovers. They stared, enraptured.

Amongst the crowd, I spotted a man I had not noticed earlier. He wore an elegant suit made of rich-looking blue cloth with silver buttons, trimmed with ermine. His long, blond, almost silver, hair fell over his shoulders. He stood with both hands on his walking stick in front of him. He wore a soft smile on his face. When I met his eyes, he bowed slightly toward me. I paused a moment, nearly forgetting myself. Then I turned back to Titania's duties. Blowing a kiss, I cast the last enchantment on the lovers. When I was done, my faeries and I moved offstage to allow Puck the final scene.

Robert exited the stage just behind me. He pulled me into a hug. "What a Titania," he whispered.

I felt the heat of a blush stinging my cheeks. It was one thing to be flattered by the audience, but a compliment from an established actor like Robert was truly an honor.

Backstage, we waited as Puck finished his closing lines: "If we shadows have offended, think but this and all is mended, that you have but slumbered here while these visions did appear…" and on until his final call of "…give me your applause if we are friends. And Robin shall make amends."

At that, the crowd broke out into wild applause.

Marve gave a signal, then Skippy dropped the curtain. Then, we waited. The crowd whistled, cheered, and clapped. Grinning happily at one another, we waited until the curtain was lifted once again then returned to the stage to soak in the accolades.

The moment I stepped onto the stage, the crowd broke out into wild cheers and rose to their feet.

"Titania! Titania!"

The crowd whistled and clapped.

I looked toward Kai. He smiled, looking genuinely happy, then bowed to me. My eyes fixed on him, I curtseyed in return. Looking over the crowd, I noticed that the fair foreign gentleman in blue was gone. And still, John was nowhere to be found.

We made our final bow, then the curtain closed for the last time. We all headed away from the theatre to the tent behind it which served as our backstage dressing area. I linked my arms with my fellow actresses, Lizzie and Amy. "Well done, fair mortals," I told the girls.

"Oh, Elyse, we are sure to lose you from the company after that performance. Did you see who was in the crowd?" Lizzie asked.

"The foreign gentleman in the blue coat? The fair one?"

"Who? No. I didn't see any fair gentleman, did you?" Lizzie asked Amy.

"Only Elyse's friend, Doctor Murray," Amy replied with a laugh, referring to Kai.

They both giggled.

I shook my head. "Who was here?"

"The stage manager from the Theatre-Royal in Covent Garden," Lizzie exclaimed excitedly.

I gasped. "I missed a line in act four!"

Lizzie shook her head. "Surely no one noticed. They were too busy watching you *be* Titania, not just act her. Elyse, I dare say, you'll be on the stage at the Theatre-Royal in no time."

"Come now, girls. We all have our gifts. The two of you did an excellent job tonight. Your argument became so heated I thought you might truly scratch each other's eyes out."

Lizzie laughed. "Elyse," she said then shook her head.

Amy patted my arm.

"Miss Elyse, a gentleman is waiting at the front for you. He sent these," said Skippy, one of the stagehands, pressing a bouquet of flowers toward me. They were roses, but they were the oddest blue color. Their tips were covered in crystalline frost.

"Frost Fair roses," Amy exclaimed. "A Spanish ship frozen in the river is selling its cargo. They were lavender, or so someone at The Frozen Mermaid said, but the cold turned them blue. Look at the tips. They're so beautiful."

John. Sweet John. Thank you.

I pulled two roses from the bouquet and handed them to each of the girls.

"Oh no, we couldn't," Lizzie objected, but she and Amy took the roses all the same, smiling at them in admiration.

"Couldn't what?" Marion, who'd played Hippolyta, asked, coming up from behind them.

I forced myself not to frown. Marion was one of the senior actresses in our company. She was very talented, and she knew it. But she was also grim and had no love for anyone else in our troupe. She was already re-dressed in her regular clothes. Had she even come on stage for curtain call?

"Someone sent Elyse Frost Fair roses," Amy explained.

Marion scrunched up her nose. "Frozen roses. They'll wilt the moment you take them inside."

"Don't be rude, Marion," Lizzie said, glaring at her.

I tried not to let her rough manner unnerve me. "For Hippolyta," I said, handing one of the blossoms to her. "For your excellent performance."

She rolled her eyes and took the blossom absently. Without another word, she left.

"Cankerblosson," Amy snarled playfully in Marion's wake. "Now, who are they from?"

"Lord Waldegrave, of course," Lizzie replied.

The girls giggled.

"Perhaps I should go find out," I said, arching my eyebrows playfully.

They nodded in agreement.

We all headed into the tent to change out of our costumes. I went to my section of the tent which had been partitioned off. Inside, straw had been laid on the floor. My trunk of full of costumes waited. A mirror sat on a barrel, a box with my makeup inside. Shivering in the cold air, I changed quickly.

I must have overlooked John in the crowd. There were so many people, so many faces there. A fleeting thought passed through my mind that perhaps the roses had come from the manager of the Theatre-Royal. For a brief moment, I closed my eyes and envisioned myself on such an elaborate stage. Certainly, Struthers Theatre was a fine enough venue, and I'd been there since my grandmother had introduced me to Marve almost five years ago, but it wasn't the Theatre-Royal. I envisioned the well-dressed lords and ladies in their boxes. Everywhere, and everything, in that theatre glimmered under the massive crystal chandelier. I envisioned myself center stage in a proper ballet costume with my pink slippers shimmering under the theatre lights. No, that dream was too big. Winning a lord with my pretty face was far more likely.

Sighing, I slipped on my coat then headed out.

"Goodnight, Elyse," Marve said. He was standing between the dressing tent and the stage lighting a pipe. "Very well done."

"Thank you. Are you spending the night on the ice?"

He nodded. "Hobbs, Robert, me, and my pistol."

The Frost Fair was certainly festive, but also highly unregulated. By now the city would have assigned some officials to keep watch over the festivities, but still, it didn't pay to take chances with the Struthers Theatre's goods.

"Can I go get you some dinner, something to drink?" I offered.

Marve shook his head. "I sent Skippy along. It was a good show. You played very well tonight."

"Like an angel?"

"Exactly like an angel."

I laughed. "Goodnight, Marve."

"Night. See you bright and early tomorrow, right?"

"Of course."

I waved then headed toward the front of the theatre. The moon was high in the sky, but the Thames was anything but dark. Torches and braziers illuminated the ice with orange light. As I turned the corner, I eyed the small crowd gathered there. Where was John?

Suddenly, a boy ran up to me. "Miss McKenna?" he asked, tugging on my arm.

"Yes?"

"A message," he said, handing me a slip of paper.

Confused, I opened the paper to find a note. The message was from John. He'd been called away on urgent business. He had to miss the show but promised to return tomorrow afternoon.

"Elyse?" Kai's voice pulled me away as I read the hastily-written lines for the fourth time. "Elyse?" he asked again, his voice softening. He set his hand on my arm. "Ah, good. You got the roses."

I looked up at my old friend. In light of the nearby torch fire, his hazel-colored eyes shimmered green.

"The...the roses?"

Kai studied my face then frowned. "What's wrong?"

I suddenly felt embarrassed. "Nothing. I'm fine. The roses are from you?"

"Did you like them?"

I smiled down at the bundle in my arms. "They're beautiful. But they're so very expensive. You shouldn't have wasted your money on me."

Kai looked perplexed. He shrugged. "I'm glad you liked them. Your performance was…Elyse, you were wonderful. This was your best show yet."

"Better than my Ophelia?"

"By far. Ophelia is too sad for you. A half-fey thing yourself, Titania fits you better. Now, come on. I'll buy you dinner. Or, at least, I'll try. I think half of the men at the Frost Fair are in love with you."

I laughed. "Then let's go to The Frozen Mermaid and see how many pints my pretty face can win us."

Kai smiled then looped his arm in mine. "You really were wonderful."

"Flatterer."

"When have you known me to flatter anyone?"

"Never."

"Then that should tell you something," he said, then led us toward the pub.

I smiled at him. As we stepped away from the theatre, I noticed something lying on the ground. I looked down to see a single Frost Fair rose lying there, the pale blue petals crushed and scattered on the snow-covered ice.

"Pity," Kai said, following my glance.

I frowned but said nothing even though I knew where the discarded blossom had come from: Marion.

I cast a glance back at the theatre. John had missed my best performance. Well, there would be others. I hoped he was all right. Something important must have pulled him away. Otherwise, why would he leave like that? A pang of doubt racked my heart, but I pushed it away. There was no room for doubt in love. I turned my attention back to the moment and smiled up at Kai, who was beaming down at me.

"Truly, a wonderful performance," he said, patting my hand. Then we turned and headed toward the festivities.

3
THE FROZEN MERMAID

THE THOROUGHFARE BETWEEN THE TENTS, dubbed Freeze-land Lane, was crowded. It seemed like all of London had come out to play on the frozen Thames. It had been years since the river had frozen solid, but this winter had been exceptionally cold. The water running under London Bridge moved so slowly that the ice had jammed, allowing the rest of the river to freeze. Out of inconvenience, an impromptu carnival on the ice was born.

"Do you want some ice cream?" Kai asked, motioning to a stand where a woman whipped cream and currants together. Several drums of the ice cream in all flavors sat on the ice keeping cool. A crowd of children gathered around.

"Honey," one called.

"Lemon," another shouted.

The workers spooned the frozen confections into small bowls.

I shook my head. "I'm already cold enough. You?"

"The same. Oysters?" he asked, pointing to another stall.

I wrinkled up my nose, catching the briny scent on the breeze. "I've been dreaming of a glass of mulled wine since act three."

Kai grinned. "The tavern it is then."

We moved down the icy path toward the tavern. Rowdy laughter abounded. We passed vendors selling roasted nuts, hot oil cakes, coffee, and hot chocolate. People pushed past, many of them on ice skates, pulling sleds heaped with goods. Gaming tents thronged with people playing dice or taking their chance at the Wheel of Fortune.

"Look," I said, grabbing Kai by the arm as we passed a group of artisans carving sculptures out of ice.

"Ah, yes. They've been working since this morning on their creations. See," Kai said, pointing to the tent which housed the makeshift tavern called The Frozen Mermaid. Sitting just outside the tent door was a mermaid carved entirely of ice.

I smiled. "I'm freezing. Let's go get some wine."

Kai nodded, and we headed inside.

"Titania!" one of the patrons called when I entered.

His attention stirred the rest of the crowd who looked at Kai and me. The crowd erupted in whistles and cheers.

I waved to them, feeling my cheeks redden with pride. It was one thing to get applause at the theatre, but being recognized out of costume was surely a sign of some skill, I hoped. My stomach knotted with butterflies.

"See, you're the most famous actress on the ice," Kai teased.

I rolled my eyes at him. "There," I said, spotting a table for the two of us at the back.

Even though there were braziers inside to ward off the chill, it was still desperately cold. I slipped into my seat and rubbed my hands together, blowing on my fingertips.

"Your nose is red," Kai said.

"You'd think I've been swimming in wine all night."

Kai smiled. "Then we best get you started."

The barmaid came to our table. "Drinks?"

"Let's begin with two mulled wines," Kai told her.

The girl smiled coquettishly at him. "As you wish, sir."

I rolled my eyes. It had almost become commonplace to see the girls flirt shamelessly with Kai. Of course, he was handsome, but the physician's bag also worked as bait. He was an excellent catch. But what they didn't know was that he seemed to have no intentions of marrying. Though women always flirted with him, I wasn't sure he even noticed.

"How did the rest of the performers do? Did you like the play?" I asked.

Kai nodded. "The Rude Mechanicals were amusing. Hippolyta, however, was far too serious. You did a very fine job, but they didn't let you dance enough."

"There's hardly any dancing in Shakespeare."

"I thought, perhaps, Lord Waldegrave would come see you perform," Kai said. I couldn't help but hear the stiffness in his voice.

John and I had, albeit covertly, been seeing one another for the last two months. He'd spotted me in a showing of *Hamlet* and was, at least per his own accord, enchanted at once.

"He was there before the performance but was called away at the last moment," I said, pulling the note from inside my sleeve where I'd stashed it. I handed it to Kai.

Kai read the note—twice—then slid it back across the table to me. Hooking his thumb under his chin, he curled his finger on his lips and looked pensive.

"Don't say anything," I told him. "It's not what you're thinking. John isn't like that."

"Like what?"

"A rake."

"Elyse, you are beautiful and talented. And despite the fact that you are also stubborn and relentless, I am sure many young men will see beyond those flaws," he said, trying to lighten the mood before he added, "but as much as I esteem you, you are also below Lord Waldegrave's station. Even a hint at an inappropriate association with you would tarnish his reputation. Surely you must—"

"That's not true. Actresses marry above their stations all the time. Last year, Miss Prynn, an actress from the Lyceum Theatre, married Lord Roberts. And two years back, an actress at the Adelphi caught the eye of a Bohemian gentleman. They, too, were married."

"I'm not bringing this up to hurt you. I just want you to be caut—"

"Here you are," the barmaid said, setting down our cups. She lingered an extra moment to smile at Kai before walking away, swinging her hips in an obvious fashion. She looked back over her shoulder at Kai, frowning when she saw he was not looking in her direction.

"You were saying?" I bit my lip. Kai was right. John had asked me to keep our liaison a secret—for now. But it still hurt to hear it, and especially to hear it from Kai, whose opinion mattered most to me.

"I just want to protect your heart. Forget I mentioned it. Now, let's toast. Cheers to your excellent performance," he said, lifting his cup.

I clinked my mug against his. "And to your health."

We both drank. I let the warm wine slip down my throat. It eased the ache that lingered there after a performance. The wine had been spiced beautifully. I tasted orange, anise, and cinnamon brewed into the dark red liquid.

"The girls said the stage manager from the Theatre-Royal in Covent Garden was in the audience," I said after I swallowed.

"Excellent. Did he come backstage?" Kai asked.

I shook my head. Kai was right to ask. If the stage manager had seen something he liked, he would have inquired with Marve. But he hadn't.

"No matter. I'm sure he'll be back," Kai said, giving my hand a reassuring squeeze.

Just then, a man rushed into the tent. "I need a surgeon. Someone said Doctor Murray came in here. Doctor Murray?" the man called, looking around the tavern.

The patrons went silent.

Kai rose. "What's the matter?"

"Are you Doctor Murray?"

"Yes."

"We've found a man in the river. We thought he'd drowned. But, sir... well, you should come."

Kai dropped two coins on the table, grabbed his bag, and looked at me. "I need to—"

"I'm coming."

Kai nodded then we both turned and followed the man back into the frozen night.

4
ONION SOUP

THE YOUNG MAN WHO'D COME to fetch Kai led us from The Frozen Mermaid to a spot on the Thames away from the tents. We rushed across the ice toward a group of men who stood with torches in hand.

"Someone noticed a stick poking out of the ice. It had a cravat attached to it. A bank of ice concealed him, but his head and shoulders were just above the water."

"How long ago?" Kai asked.

"About fifteen minutes. By chance, one of the lads remembered seeing you enter The Frozen Mermaid with Miss McKenna. Sir, I'm not sure he's alive. His skin…" the man said then paused to look back at me.

"Don't worry, she's quite used to medical ministry," Kai said.

While Kai was the one who'd taken the formal training as a doctor, he never shied away from showing me what he had learned. At this point, if my career as an actress or a dancer faltered, I'd make a good physician's assistant.

"His skin was blue in the manner of death. We thought he was gone, but then he took a breath."

"Any heartbeat?"

"We couldn't tell. Some of the lads were trying to give him some Scotch to revive him."

"Fools," Kai muttered then hurried his step. I followed quickly behind him.

Kai rushed forward as we drew close. Five men stood around another man who lay on the ice. His skin had paled to an ashen color tinged with the same blue as the Frost Fair roses. The man's black hair was washed back in straight lines; the damp hair at the base of his neck appeared to be frozen to the river's icy surface. His lips were blue. The man, I noticed, wore an expensive suit. He was a gentleman of some distinction. How odd that he would be found in this condition. Kai dropped to his knees as he pulled his instruments from his bag. He did it with so swift a motion that it seemed natural. Mixed emotions of worry for the frozen man and pride in my oldest friend swelled in my heart. For many years I had watched Kai study, advancing from apothecary to surgeon, then his years in service as an apprentice until he became a doctor. I was fairly sure there was no man in London as brilliant as Kai.

"Quickly, gentlemen. Your coats," Kai called to the others. At once, each man pulled off his jacket and laid it on the frozen man as Kai pressed his ear to the man's chest, searching for a heartbeat.

Shaking his head, Kai grabbed the man's shirt and ripped it open down the front. The silver buttons snapped off the garment. They flew through the air, shimmering like diamonds, then fell on the ice, twinkling dimly in the torchlight. The effect of it enraptured me so that I stared at the brilliant pieces. A moment later, a swirl of snow rose off the surface of the Thames. It glimmered crystalline as it swept toward the buttons. The light must have struck the powdered snow just right, because amongst the frozen powder, I could have sworn I'd seen something thumb-sized and brilliant blue zipping to and fro. Perhaps the moonlight was being reflected in the swirl of snow? A moment later, however, the snow settled. When I looked once more, I realized that the silver buttons were gone. Had they been blown away?

"Shh," Kai hissed, motioning for the men to be silent.

The men muttered quietly.

Kai frowned as he strained to listen.

"Be silent, gentlemen," I told them.

Rightly chastised, they quieted.

Kai listened intently then sat up.

Frustrated, he pushed his hair back. When he went to lean in again, he spied a boy standing beside his father. The child held a cone with a ball attached.

"May I use that?" Kai asked him.

The boy nodded absently then handed the cone to Kai.

Kai set the wide part of the cone on the man's chest and gently placed his ear on the smaller end. A moment later, his eyebrows arched and a wisp of a smile crossed his face. He sat up. "There is still a chance. You," he said, turning to the boy. "Run to the soup maker. Tell her to prepare a barrel of warm water. Go quickly. This man may yet survive, but we need to move him."

"Grab his legs, boys," one of the men said to his comrades in a slurred voice.

"No," Kai said. "We need a stretcher."

The men looked around, puzzled.

"Here," I said, unfastening the tie at the neck of my long winter coat. I unbuttoned the garment and pressed it toward Kai.

Kai motioned to the men to lay my coat on the ice while he absent-mindedly pulled off his jacket. Without another word, he handed it to me. I slid into the coat. It was still warm from his body heat. I was overcome with his familiar scent. I caught a hint of the spicy shaving soap he preferred and the sharp, tangy smells of medicines. But more than that, I could smell him, the deep scent a person's body carries that you recognize with familiarity. To me, Kai's very essence carried the smells of sunshine and summer. And after a lifetime of being with him, it was an essence I knew as well as my own.

Kai moved to help the others lift the man from the ice onto my coat. I could not help but notice how the man's clothes and hair stuck to the surface of the river. The Thames seemed unwilling to let go of what she'd won.

The men dashed quickly across the ice, carrying the man toward the soup maker's tent.

"Clear the way," a man yelled, moving the crowd aside.

As we approached the tent, an old woman stepped into the lane. "Here, here," she called, motioning us forward.

We rushed ahead.

The woman directed us to a large barrel.

Kai motioned to the other men, and on the count of three, they lifted the drowned man and slid him into the barrel of warm water. The man bobbed oddly in the barrel, the water reaching his chest.

"We must heat his trunk uniformly, or the icy blood will stop his heart. Do you have anything else? Anything?" Kai asked the cook urgently.

"Kai," I said, pointing to a pot heating over a stove.

"Madame, is it boiling?" he asked her.

"No, Doctor. It's just…it's stock, beef and onions."

"Help me," Kai said and moving quickly, the three of us lifted the cauldron. Careful not to burn ourselves, the cook handling the pot with covered hands, we poured the hot broth into the barrel where the unconscious man slumped weirdly.

Keeping Kai's words in mind, I grabbed a bundle of linens from the nearby table, dashed them into the hot water, and covered the man's head with the steaming towels.

Kai stood behind the man and pressed him into the water as deeply as possible, pushing him down until just a little of his face protruded from the steaming liquid.

Bits of meat and onions bobbed at the top of the barrel.

A moment later, the man's eyelashes fluttered.

"Did you see that?" I whispered to Kai.

He nodded. "Madame, please ask the others to bring blankets and warm wraps, as many as can be spared," Kai told the cook who went to the door of her tent and relayed the request to the crowd.

"A few more minutes in the hot liquid. Then, once the wraps are here, we must get him dry and close to a hearth," Kai told me.

"He needs to get off the Thames," I said.

Kai nodded.

A moment later, Kai and I both paused when we heard the man whisper.

"Mother? Are we having onion soup?"

I suppressed a laugh.

"Sir? Sir, can you hear me?" Kai called.

The man's eyes fluttered open for a moment. A confused expression crossed his face. "I don't like onion soup," he whispered then closed his eyes once more.

I smiled gently at him and mopped his head once more with the heated cloths. "So quick bright things come to confusion," I whispered, stealing a line from Shakespeare's play.

A few minutes later, the cook returned, men following behind her carrying heaps of blankets.

"Gentlemen, please stay. Ladies, I must ask you to step out," he said, motioning to the cook and me.

"I can help," I offered.

Kai shook his head. "He must be undressed."

Nodding, I stepped outside.

A large crowd had gathered around.

"Miss? Is he dead? What's happening?" someone called.

"He did wake for just a moment, but he is not clear of danger yet," I informed them.

"Miss," the young boy, whose toy had been such aid, tugged at the sleeve of Kai's jacket. "You dropped these," he said, handing me my roses.

I bent down and kissed the boy on the forehead. "Thank you. What a help you are, young man."

He smiled. Even in the dim evening light, I could see his cheeks burn red. He bowed to me then ran off.

I waited by the brazier just outside the tent. My chest ached. I realized then that tension had racked at me. I'd been holding my breath in fits and spurts. I stared at the tent flap, wishing for Kai to reappear.

A moment later, one of the men quickly exited the tent and ran into the night. After him, another man rushed out, calling for a wagon.

Cautiously, I stepped back inside. The man lay on the table covered in blankets. His eyes were open, but he babbled incoherently.

"He's alive," Kai told me. "But his wit's diseased. I've sent a messenger to Master Hawking. It is the nearest amiable place I can think of."

I nodded but said nothing. I was very certain that amiable was an understatement of Kai's esteem for the tinker, Master Hawking, and his daughter, Isabelle.

I moved to the table where the man lay staring at some unknown point in the distance. "Does anyone know who he is?" I asked.

Kai shook his head.

"Sir, what is your name?" I asked him.

He turned and looked at me. "Titania?"

I looked up at Kai. "He must have been at the play."

"Titania, tell mother I don't like onion soup," he whispered.

"I will remind her," I said, smiling softly at him. Unsure what to do, I pulled a stool out and sat beside the man, and gently set my hand on his arm. "Shall I sing for you?" I asked.

I looked to Kai who nodded in approval as he checked the man's feet.

When the man made no other comment, I began singing lightly. An old tune my granny used to sing to me, the song of two lovers who met in secret in a rose garden, came to mind. The song, which took place in summer, reminded me of warmer days and bright sunshine. I closed my eyes and imagined bright light beaming down on the man, filling his entire body with sunshine and warmth.

It felt like an eternity passed before one of the men returned. "Master Hawking is expecting you, Doctor," the man said as he held open the tent door just as I warbled the last line of my song.

I looked past the man and outside. Amongst the crowd, I spotted the fair-haired foreign gentleman in the blue suit.

I smiled at him.

He returned my smile, tipping the brim of his top hat toward me, but then others crowded around, and I couldn't see him anymore.

Kai nodded. "The wagon?"

"Just pulled up."

"We're ready, Doctor Murray," another man called as he appeared at the tent door.

I stepped aside as the men moved to carefully carry the insensible gentleman to the wagon. It was just a short ride along the Thames to the Hawkings' workshop.

"Elyse, why don't you go home," Kai suggested, gently taking my hand in his. "Your hands are freezing. This has been quite enough for you for one night, I think."

"You may need my help," I offered.

"I may need to spend the night unless we can call in the local surgeon to look after him."

I nodded. Still, I hated to let him go alone.

Kai squeezed my hand. "Have someone walk you home."

"I will. Be safe."

Kai nodded then slid into the back of the wagon with his patient. He passed a word to the driver, then they headed down Freezeland Lane out of sight.

I stared in the distance at London Bridge. They said the old bridge was falling apart. There was already talk of tearing her down. Light shone from the gas lamps lining the bridge. From my point of view on the river, they shimmered like gaudy stars.

"Miss McKenna," the cook said.

I turned to look at her.

"How about a bowl of soup to warm you before you leave?"

I smiled and nodded. "Thank you. Yes. Anything but onion," I said with a laugh which she joined.

5

IGNORING CASSANDRA

"HERE YOU ARE, MISS MCKENNA," Old Master Williams said, slowing his carriage in front of my door. He slipped out of the carriage to help me down.

"Thank you again, sir." Taking his hand, I stepped onto the street. The fog was so thick that I couldn't see the buildings at the end of the row.

"Think nothing of it," he said with a tip of the hat. "Such strange weather, isn't it? I don't remember seeing such fog before."

I nodded. "Strange, indeed."

"You haven't enchanted it, have you, faerie queen?"

I laughed. "Perhaps. But I would never tell if I had."

The man grinned then bowed.

"Again, my thanks," I told him then reached into my reticule for my key. "Good night."

"And to you," he said then got into his carriage once more. Clicking lightly at his horse, he drove off.

Unlocking the door, I headed inside. The stairs wound upward to my small flat in the third-floor garret at the top of the building. Once inside, I set about getting my fireplace going. Grabbing a vase, I placed the Frost Fair roses close to the window. Marion's snarky, but true words came to mind. They would fade in the heat. Perhaps the chill from the window would keep them blue a bit longer. Only when the orange light filled the room, the flames fighting off the chill, did I pull off Kai's coat. I slid a chair close to the fire and slipped off my boots, setting my feet as close to the flames as I dared. I closed my eyes, soaking in the warmth. My mind drifted to thoughts of Granny. How empty the small apartment seemed without her. It had been three years since she'd died, but her touches were still everywhere. From the watercolor paintings on the wall to the embroidered pillows, I felt her presence. I wished she'd been there tonight to see the play. She would have loved it. And she would have been proud of Kai as well.

I smiled when I thought about Granny and Kai's grandmother, Gerda, whom I'd called Gram. I sighed, thinking about Granny and Gram, and looked out the window of the garret. Though the window was trimmed with ice, I spied the window frame to Kai's garret apartment. How our grandmothers used to love to sit by their windows and talk the whole day long. Though misfortune brought both Kai and me under our grandmothers' care, it had also brought us one another in the process.

My eyes drooped closed. While it was exciting to be the only players on the Thames, it had made for a long day exposed to the chill. Now, the small room was cozy and warm. As I rested, I envisioned John's estate in Twickenham with its exquisite parlors and bed chambers. My little garret was probably the size of his butler's pantry. How nice it would be to win such a fine man's heart and live in a fine house with fine things. I knew very well that actresses were often the playthings of gentlemen, but it wasn't that way with John. From the first moment I'd met him, he'd been nothing but proper.

About two months earlier, after a performance of *Hamlet*, I'd received a note that a Lord Waldegrave wanted to meet me to express his compliments.

"A lord?" Amy had said, her eyes wide, when I shared the note with the girls. Lizzie and Hannah had crowded behind me to look over my shoulder at the paper. We were in the ladies' dressing room backstage.

Marion snorted. "Not hard to guess what he's interested in. You already have a doctor. Do you need a nobleman too? And didn't you just scuttle off a different lord the other night?" she asked. While she attempted to mask it, there was no denying the envy that tinged her voice.

"First, Doctor Murray is just my friend. And yes, but that was Lord Byron, and everyone knows what he's about."

Lizzie squeezed my arm playfully. "And still you said no. Elyse, how could you? Reputation or no, Lord Byron is an Adonis. And so very famous. Even fine ladies chase him."

"Such as Lady Caroline Lamb, who went mad and attempted to take her own life over their broken affair?"

Lizzie sighed dreamily. "Yes…what passion the poet must provoke."

"Then I shall point him your direction next time, my Cassandra-like warnings unheeded."

Lizzie laughed.

Marion rolled her eyes, picked up her coat, and left.

"Lord Waldegrave. That name is not familiar to me." I looked at the other girls, who shrugged. What did we, low-born as we were, know of lords? Many dazzling names circled the aether over our heads. Only because Byron was so scandalous, and well known amongst the London actresses for his carousing, was he well-noted. Lord Waldegrave? I had no idea who he was. "Well, I shall meet him and see. Knowing my luck, he is some merry old curmudgeon, and I remind him of his granddaughter."

At that, the girls laughed. Chatting merrily amongst themselves, they quickly changed then left the theatre.

I sat down at my dressing table and looked into the mirror. I was tired. I had been ill with a fever over Christmas and had just recovered. My already pale skin looked whiter than usual, and the performance had drained me. I hardly would have tried a role as taxing as Ophelia except Marion had commented that I wasn't good enough for the part.

I quickly removed my stage makeup and fixed my hair. I had worn a simple day gown to the theatre that day, not thinking I would be seeing anyone other than Kai after the performance. Though he was often busy working, Kai would always meet me after a performance to walk me home. I slipped on my plum-colored dress. While it was hardly fashionable, the color was flattering. I took my pelisse from the peg and headed back into the theatre. I paused a moment when I got to the empty stage. Aside from Marve and Skippy, there was no one left at the Struthers Theatre. The seats were all vacant, and only a few lights glowed. I set down my basket and coat. Taking just a moment before I headed to the lobby, I closed my eyes and breathed in the stage.

The scent of the timbers, the dust, the smell of the upholstery, the perfume that was the stage filled my nose. I closed my eyes and centered myself. Then, wanting to feel the joy of it for just a moment, I moved into first position then pirouetted across the stage. Grabbing my skirt and lifting it a bit to free my legs, I turned and danced a petit allegro. The joy I felt in the movements, the quick leaps, which I felt landed in perfect succession, filled my heart with joy.

When I was finished, I smiled widely then exhaled deeply, my breath quickening at the task.

I was taken by surprise, however, when applause came from the audience.

I looked into the darkened theatre and spotted a gentleman wearing a green coat walking toward the stage.

"Forgive me, Miss McKenna, isn't it?" he asked, removing his top hat. "I was in the lobby when I realized I'd forgotten my walking stick," he said, stepping into a row of seats to retrieve the stick. "I did not mean to intrude."

My cheeks flushed red. It was one thing to be seen on the stage when you were expecting it. It was quite another to dance, unbridled, legs over-exposed. Trying to hide my embarrassment, I smiled confidently, picked up my basket and headed down the steps into the house.

"I'm afraid you have the better of me," I said, curtseying politely when I met the gentleman mid-aisle.

He bowed. "Lord John Waldegrave."

No, no elderly curmudgeon. A tall man about my age with reddish brown hair, soft brown eyes, and a very nice cut, Lord Waldegrave was a handsome young gentleman.

"Pleased to make your acquaintance. I'm Elyse McKenna. Shall we remove to the lobby? The lighting is dreadful here." And it was very inappropriate to meet with his lordship in a darkened theatre.

He nodded, and we headed toward the front of the house.

"Miss McKenna, I am astounded at the range of your skills. I knew you to be a talented actress. I hadn't known you were also gifted in ballet."

My cheeks reddened again. "I am not formally trained, sir. My grandmother, however, was a ballerina. She taught me."

"I must apologize for intruding again. But I must admit, it was a delight to watch. Do you perform ballet elsewhere?"

"No," I said, suddenly feeling embarrassed. In truth, it was tough to gain the attention of a larger, more famous company. I was settled with my troupe, but my heart still aspired higher.

"Well," he said, seeming to understand the problem, "I am confident that given time, you will catch the attention of anyone who is able to recognize natural talent." Lord Waldegrave opened the door, and we entered the lobby. "Do you perform every night?" he asked.

I nodded. "Yes."

"And during the day?"

"We vary our matinees. At present, I am not on the stage on Tuesdays and Thursdays."

"I..." he began, then twisted his hat in his hands. "Might I call on you? This Thursday?"

I bit the inside of my cheek. There was no way I could accept such a fine gentleman caller at my garret apartment. Aside from that, I had no proper chaperone. A girl who didn't care much about her reputation would have accepted the invitation with no regard to either. But I was not such a girl, and I wanted to make that abundantly clear.

"I'm afraid...I do not have...You see, my home...Lord Waldegrave, I'm afraid I—" I began then burst out laughing at the absurdity of the situation. I covered my mouth with my hands then looked at him.

He smiled softly, seeming to understand. "Miss McKenna, may I propose that we take a tour of the British Museum this Thursday? I can meet you there, perhaps?"

I exhaled a sigh of relief. "Thank you. I would love that."

With a bow, Lord Waldegrave put on his top hat once more. "It was a pleasure to meet you. I look forward to seeing you on Thursday," he said, and with a smile, he exited the lobby.

I stood a moment trying to catch my breath.

"I am amazed and know not what to say," I said to no one in particular, snatching a line from Shakespeare's Hermia. He had understood my situation and had, in the kindest of ways, sought to remedy my discomfort. And with that, his behavior suggested that this gentleman was not merely looking for carnal entertainment. I scarcely knew what to think.

I slipped on my pelisse. I was buttoning it up when Kai entered the lobby.

"Ah, sorry I'm late. The Haughton's son had a terrible cough. How was it?"

"Amazing."

"Amazing?"

"You won't believe what just happened," I said then shared the exchange with Kai, whose face grew darker, or so it seemed, with my every word.

"Go cautiously. He may be ill-intended."

"Must you assume the worst of everyone?"

"Seems prudent to do so."

"Perhaps I'm so ugly that you can't imagine a fine man courting me?" I teased.

"On the contrary. I can imagine all men, fine or not, trying to court you. That's what has me worried."

"You jest."

"Do I?" he said. "No. I worry. Such a man cannot court you without scandal. So either he is braced for a liaison that may call into question his reputation or he doesn't have honest intentions."

"Kai," I said in an exhausted huff. I reached out and tickled his ribs. He yelped, evoking a boyish squeal.

I giggled.

"Don't do that again," Kai said with a smile, snatching hold my hand to prevent me from pestering him again.

"Or what?"

"Or I'll forbid you from meeting your fancy gentleman."

"And just how do you propose to enforce that?"

"Hum," Kai said then looked thoughtful. "I'll find a way."

I blew air through my lips. "Instead, wish me well."

"You know I do. Speaking of, how are you feeling? Is the performance taxing you too much?"

"A little, but I'll never admit it to anyone but you."

"Be sure you rest tonight. You're just getting well."

I squeezed Kai's hand, grateful that he watched over me as he always had.

My mind drifted back to the present. If John formed a genuine attachment to me, if there was a chance I could marry him, then what?

What of Kai? He had been in my life all my life. How would I live without Kai across from my window? As I drifted off to sleep, a single thought pricked at my heart. How could I live without Kai?

IT WAS SOME TIME IN the middle of the night when I heard the latch on my window rattle. Sleepy eyed, having been lost in a dream, I looked up. A moment later, the panes opened, letting in a gust of cold winter wind. Feet first, Kai slipped into my flat.

I smiled sleepily at him. "What time is it?"

"Nearly three o'clock."

"You're just getting in now?"

"Obviously," he said with a grin. Kneeling before my fireplace, he banked up the flames.

"How is the gentleman?"

"Alive. He's still out of his mind, but his heart is steady, and the color has come back to his extremities. The local surgeon will look after him for a few days. Master Hawking was very obliging."

"He's a kind man," I said, feeling my eyes shut once more. "I'd like to visit the gentleman tomorrow. Will you take me when you go?"

"Of course. Are you performing in the morning?"

"At ten. I'll play the role of the faerie godmother in the morning pantomime."

"Fitting."

"The godmother and not the maiden? Have I lost my bloom already?"

Kai smiled. "Hardly. By playing the faerie once more, you'll steep yourself in a mystique for the fairgoers."

"Mystique. I like that."

Kai covered me with a thick blanket. "You should get into your cot."

"I'm far too comfortable here. You take it. It will take too long for you to get your fire going at this time of night."

"Stay here? Are you certain? It's not entirely prop—"

"Proper, proper, always on with what is proper. Kai, you are like my own blood and know me as well as I know myself. Since we were children—"

"But we aren't children anymore. And we are not brother and sister."

"Indeed. But who knows you are here save the mice and me? Stop arguing with me and lie down. I'm going back to my dream."

Kai sighed then I heard the frame of my cot creak as it took on his weight. "What were you dreaming about?"

"I was in a forest. It was very green."

"Most forests are."

"Tease. I mean, it was very green, lush, with leaves and flowers galore, and someone was playing a harp. People were dancing around a maypole," I said with a yawn, feeling myself slip back to sleep.

"Sounds nice. I'll try to meet you there."

I chuckled, or at least I tried to, as I was half asleep once more. "Nosy boy. Go have your own dreams."

"Yours are much better than mine. And I want to see you dance in the forest, nymph."

"Rogue."

Kai laughed softly. "Goodnight, Elyse."

"Goodnight, Kai."

6

THE INGENIOUS
(AND ATTRACTIVE)
MISS ISABELLE HAWKING

THE FOLLOWING MORNING, AFTER WE shared breakfast, Kai retreated to his flat to get ready for the day. I closed the curtains on the garret window, refreshed myself, and then waited for Kai. As I sat at my small kitchen table stirring my tea, I wondered for the hundredth time why Kai still kept a residence in his little garret apartment. He didn't have the money for anything better when he was an apprentice, but now that he earned a doctor's wages, he could afford a modest home. Indeed, if he went into the country, he would likely be able to find a position and fine house. I frowned. Was he, like me, attached to the space out of sentiment?

I heard a tap at the window.

Kai and I kept an endless supply of pebbles at the window sill. I rose and went to the window. Pushing the curtains aside, I expected to see Kai leaning out his window waiting for me. Instead, I found a mourning dove on the ledge. When I opened the curtains, I startled the poor creature, and it flew away, leaving behind what I'd thought was a twig. Then I noticed a splash of purple color. I opened the window and discovered that the twig was not a twig at all but a lovely spring crocus, deep purple and vibrant yellow in color.

I turned to call to Kai when I noticed that his window was still shut. I looked through the glass and caught sight of him as he buttoned the top of his trousers. Shirtless, he stood adjusting his trousers. His undershirt and shirt sat on the chair nearby. I moved to go back inside but paused a moment. I hadn't remembered Kai being so fit. Granted, it had been years since I'd seen Gram scrub him down, complaining that he smelled of dirt, but I had not realized he was so muscular. His chest had a smattering of dark hair. His stomach was firm. Trailing down from his belly button was a line of dark hair that led to—

Gasping, surprised by and embarrassed of, myself, I closed the window. I felt my cheeks redden. I closed my eyes and tried to shut out the images that played across my mind. The thought of Kai naked had made my heart quicken.

"Elyse, you need to get married soon before you sully your virtue," I berated myself as I pushed the last of the lustful thoughts away.

Keeping myself busy, I turned to examine the Frost Fair roses. Overnight, they had warmed to a pale purple color. The smell coming off the blossoms was heavenly.

A few moments later, I heard a tap on my window once more. I waited, listening for a second tap. This time I wanted to be certain it was Kai's call before I called my modesty into question again. A stone tapped on the window again.

I opened the curtains. Kai was leaning in the opposite window frame. I pushed open the latch.

"Romeo, Romeo, wherefore art thou, Romeo?" I called lightly, making Kai smile.

"Are you ready, Juliet?"

"I am."

"You know they both die in that play, right?"

I laughed. "But what a romance first. Meet you below?"

Kai nodded.

I latched the window then turned and pulled on my heavy jacket. Bundled in layers of clothing, I headed outside.

By the time I got downstairs, Kai was already waiting for me. As always, he carried his doctor's bag. Offering me his arm, we headed out. A light snow had started to fall. Given it was early morning, the new dust covered everything with a beautiful shimmer of white.

As we headed in the direction of London Bridge, I said, "Kai, I was thinking—"

"Oh dear. So much mischief has always followed those words."

"Not always."

"Kai, I was thinking, why don't we make dinner for our grannies? Kai, I was thinking, should we try to crawl down the drain spout? Kai, I was thinking you would look very fetching without any hair. Let me see: fire, a broken arm, and a bald head, complete with several small cuts, which also earned me a switching."

I laughed. "Yes, but wasn't it the broken arm which introduced you to Doctor Thompson who later supported you in your studies? You see, if it weren't for me, you would never have studied medicine."

"Because you talked me into breaking my arm?"

"I did not talk you into breaking your arm. And if it had worked, sliding down the drain spout *would* have been much faster than the stairs. But anyway, I was thinking, why do you still live in the flat? I mean, it's not my business, but haven't you saved enough from your practice to afford a nicer home? Something larger? In a better neighborhood?"

I felt Kai's muscles tense under my arm. "I have been saving my money, you are right. And I do have enough saved so I could do as you suggest. But…"

"But?"

"Now is not the time."

"I see."

Kai laughed lightly. "You see, meaning that you will think it over then quiz me later."

"Precisely. You know, it's very annoying that I'm so predictable."

"Only to me."

"That's true. John has told me that I am very clever. He finds it quite surprising and not at all predictable," I said teasingly.

"Interesting. Your wit doesn't come as a surprise to me at all," Kai said stiffly.

"He doesn't mean it the way you are suggesting."

"No. I'm sure he doesn't."

"You know, you could try to like him."

"I could. But I will wait to ensure that I *should* first."

"Kai, you are a grumpy old bear," I said, reaching up to ruffle his dark hair sticking out just from under the back of his top hat.

He grinned then caught my fingers. "It's not wise to provoke a bear," he said, setting the lightest of kisses on my gloved fingers before he returned my hand to me.

It was a movement he must have made a hundred times in the past, a familiarity I'd never thought anything of before, but given my immodest thoughts, the gesture struck me oddly. I felt a strange stirring in my stomach.

"Careful here," Kai said, setting his hand on my lower back as he guided me around a patch of ice.

"Thank you," I replied nicely.

Kai smiled. "Of course."

We worked our way through the streets until we reached London

Bridge. Turning down the narrow riverside road, we soon came to the home and workshop of Master Hawking.

Kai rang for the footman while I looked out on the frozen Thames. Already the river was busy with activity. I still had time, however, before I needed to join my company to prepare the morning's performance. And I hoped, above all, that John would come today. I hated to think that something had happened to him.

"Doctor Murray. Do come in," I heard the footman say.

Turning, I joined them.

"Master Hawking is in his workshop. I'll inform him you're here."

"Is the surgeon still here?" Kai asked as we entered.

"Yes, sir. Miss Hawking convinced him to stay for breakfast. He is in the dining room."

Kai nodded, and we followed the footman to the parlor. The room, while properly adorned, reminded me much of the rest of Master Hawkings' home, which I had visited but twice before—full of his tinkered contraptions. On the wall, a framed picture depicting a waterfall ticked like a clock as blue-colored balls rolled down the river and over the waterfall. The effect of the moving image was enchanting. An elaborate grandfather clock stood at one end of the room. Rather than having a single face, the clock showed several times in several locations from London to Constantinople to Bombay to New York City and even more. Every piece of furniture was stacked with books. I smiled when I realized that there was nowhere to sit.

"Look," Kai said then turned the windup key on what looked like a music box. A moment later, the box opened to reveal a stage. Metal drapes drew back to reveal a tiny clockwork ballerina. The ballerina pirouetted via a groove in the metal. Music played, giving an added grace to her steps.

I gasped.

"Miss Hawking has been working on pairing clockwork and tone. I believe this is one of her works."

I was about to reply when a voice interrupted me.

"Indeed it is," a man called.

I turned to find Master Hawking. Dressed in a wool suit covered by a leather apron, it appeared that the tinker had already been hard at work that morning.

"Good morning, Doctor Murray. And Miss McKenna. Always a pleasure to see you," Master Hawking said.

"Sir," I replied, curtseying.

Master Hawking smiled.

"You must be here to see your patient. Shall we?" Master Hawking said, motioning to the stairs.

Kai nodded to me, indicating I should follow.

"I'm sure my footman informed Mister Blackwell that you're here. We'll have him come up after breakfast. Your drowned man slept well through the night. He had a spot of tea and bread with jam this morning."

"Have his senses returned?"

Master Hawking shook his head. "I'm afraid not." He led us to the door of a bedchamber then knocked on the door.

A maid appeared.

"Is he awake?"

"Yes, sir."

"Very good," Master Hawking said then motioned for us to follow him.

The man who had quite nearly drowned the evening before was sitting upright in bed. He'd been changed into a nightdress. To my surprise, he appeared much younger than he had the night before. Apparently being near-death gave one the hue of middle-age, which did not speak well, of course, of the middle years. This morning, I would guess him to be a man in his late twenties. The fire in the room burned brightly. In my outdoor wraps, the room felt over-warm. Kai must have thought the same as he loosened the top button of his jacket. The man was sipping a cup of tea, which he set aside when we entered.

"Sir," Kai said, nodding politely to him. "Do you remember me?"

The man coughed in an attempt to clear his throat. He motioned for us to wait a moment as he sipped his tea once more, then he said, "Yes, sir. I believe you are the doctor to whom I owe my life."

Kai bowed his head politely. "I am Doctor Murray."

The man looked around Kai and stared at me. "I...I know you, I think," he told me.

"This is Miss Elyse McKenna," Kai introduced.

The man furrowed his brow. "Onion soup," he said then shook his head. "But I do recall you from elsewhere. Sounds silly, but I keep thinking of faeries," he said with an awkward smile.

"I am an actress, sir. We believe you saw me perform yesterday night before your accident. I was playing the role of Titania at the Ice House Theatre on the Thames."

The man lifted the cup of tea and took a sip. "Yes. I…I do remember something of the play."

"Something of it?"

"I remember you kissing…pardon me, Miss. I don't mean to be rude, and I know this sounds absurd, but I remember you kissing a donkey. That, and onion soup."

I smiled. "There is no offense on your part, sir. It is Master Shakespeare who is at fault."

The man chuckled.

"Miss McKenna, I would like to examine Mister…our guest," Kai told me.

"Master Hawking, perhaps you would be kind enough to take me to your daughter?" I said, turning to the tinker.

He nodded, and I followed him out of the room.

Kai closed the door behind us.

"Poor chap," Master Hawking said as we headed back downstairs. "The

Thames took his memory, but it seems she was cold enough to save his life."

"What do you mean?"

"Ah, well, a man may fall into the water and die of cold, that is certain, but if the water is frozen enough, cold enough, his body goes into a kind of slumber."

"How very odd."

"Isn't it? Now, my daughter is in her workshop. This way," Master Hawking said, leading me toward the back of the house.

Opening a set of double doors, Master Hawking led me into a room that appeared to be half library, half workshop. Tables were heaped with cogs and contraptions, tools and wire, and books were strewn everywhere. There was a sharp clatter followed by a stream of obscenities in a distinctly feminine voice.

"Isabelle?" Master Hawking called, peering around the room. "Doctor Murray's friend, Miss Elyse McKenna, is here to see you."

"Doctor Murray is here?" I heard the girl exclaim with the tone of excitement. Metal clattered once more.

"Yes, and his friend, Miss McKenna."

A moment later, the girl appeared before me. Wearing a wool skirt, a long-sleeved shirt, and a leather apron, the girl was dressed to work. She pushed a pair of goggles onto her head then wiped a gloved hand across her chin, leaving a smear of grease in its wake. With her long, dark-brown braid and wide brown eyes, she was decidedly attractive.

"Miss McKenna," she chirped, curtsying to me. "So nice to see you again. I have to apologize," she said, motioning to her dress. "I was working. Would you like to see?"

"Oh yes," I replied.

"Very good," Master Hawking said. "I'll leave you to it then. Miss McKenna," he said, nodding politely, then he excused himself.

Miss Hawking waved to me to follow her. "You're just in time, in fact. I was filing down the last bit. Nearly broke the piece, but cut me instead," she said, looking at her finger, which was wrapped in cloth stained with blood.

"Are you all right?"

"Fine, fine. Just made me mad. Come see. You'll be the very first!"

She led me to her workbench. There, I saw the amazing sculpture she'd been working on. She'd sculpted a tree branch from metal, and on it sat six little songbirds.

"Oh, it's so lovely," I told her.

"Wait," she said. She reached forward and pressed down on one of the leaves. A moment later, the birds began to warble. One at a time, they chirped gaily.

I clasped my hands together. "That's—" I began, but she lifted a finger for me to wait once more and pressed another leaf.

A moment later, the birds began in earnest, warbling out Vivaldi's *Allegro-Largo-Allegro*. I stood staring at the little birds as they chirped in chorus, turning their heads and ruffling the wings and tail feathers as they vocalized the first minute of the piece. A moment later, they went silent. They shook their metal bodies as if roosting and settled into place once more.

"I'm still working on a way to integrate the full movement, but this is a start. What do you think?" Isabelle asked, turning to me.

I stared wide-eyed at her.

She laughed. "You like it, then?"

"Miss Hawking, you're quite brilliant."

"Papa is the brilliant one. He's working on quite serious projects. A clockwork eye, for example," she said, motioning to the workbench behind her where several metal and glass eyes lay scattered. "I'm more for frivolity."

"You do remember that you're talking to an actress."

She laughed. "And ballerina. Or so I was told."

"Yes. My grandmother was a dancer in her youth. She taught me. All my gifts come from her effort and patience."

Isabelle smiled, but I noticed a sadness to her smile, and I recognized it. It is the smile of a girl who was raised without a mother. "And mine from Papa's."

"Well, this work is stunning," I said, turning back to the birds. "You'll need to show this to Kai—Doctor Murray."

"Do you think he'll like it?" she asked, her expression brightening. "It's so hard to know what pleases him. He's always so dour."

I smiled at her, looking at her once more in a new light. She was, perhaps, seventeen or so. Was she looking for a husband? Kai would be a fine catch for a quirky tinker's daughter. And he could certainly appreciate a clever and talented girl, whereas others might find her lacking in manners. Perhaps it would be a good match. Perhaps, except the idea of it made something in my stomach harden.

"I'm sure he will."

Miss Hawking set her gloves on the table then turned her attention back to the birds, but I could see that even as she spoke, she was distracted. "I'm not quite done with them yet. I'll add colored glass for the eyes and just a bit of color on the leaves."

"Is it a commission?"

She nodded. "A wedding gift. Some Scottish lord ordered it. I still have time. The wedding is not until May."

"What a lovely gift."

"Elyse?" I heard Kai call from the front of the workshop.

"I'm here, Doctor Murray," I called, reminding Kai that we were not alone.

I heard him cough. "Yes. Right. Miss McKenna. Is Miss Hawking here?"

Miss Hawking leaped away from her table. On second thought, however, she pulled off her goggles, removed her apron, and smoothed her long wool skirt.

Her primping was not lost on me. Pulling a handkerchief from my bag, I handed it to her. "Your chin," I said. I really did need to carry a hand mirror.

Smiling at me in a very sisterly way, she tidied up, handing me the soiled handkerchief, then headed back toward the door. I hid my frown as I tucked the cloth back inside my bag. It was going to take a hard soaking to get that grease out.

"Doctor Murray," she called with a wave.

To my surprise, Kai brightened when he saw her.

Once more, that strange knot formed in my stomach.

"Miss Hawking. How are you this morning?"

"Very well."

"I was just checking on my patient."

"He's a very amiable man. You know, I think he might be a gentleman of some station."

"Why do you say that?"

"Well," she said, looking a bit embarrassed. "It seems best for a lady to show refined conduct around him so as not to upset his sensibilities," she said with a cough. "But aside from that, it was his manner. He's clearly well-educated, sophisticated, and he ate very properly. And he commented on our sugar. He was confused as to why the sugar wasn't white."

I shook my head and looked at Kai.

"The wealthy use refined white sugar," Kai explained.

"Oh," I said, suddenly feeling foolish for not knowing. Lady Waldegrave

I certainly was not.

"Mister Blackwell said he filed a report with the Bow Street Runners on the gentleman's behalf. Have they been by?"

Miss Hawking shook her head.

"Perhaps later. If he is a man of consequence, someone will be looking for him."

"What a funny thing to say," Miss Hawking said then.

"Why?"

"Well, he need not be a man of consequence for someone to miss him."

Kai nodded. "Quite right. I guess I was just thinking—"

Miss Hawking laughed. "I only jest. I understood your meaning. Now, if you have a moment more, may I show you my latest creation?"

Kai nodded.

I followed behind them as Miss Hawking led Kai to her workstation. As she had with me, she delighted him with her design. Staying a bit back, I watched the exchange with curiosity. Miss Hawking's eyes almost never left Kai's face as she hunted for a sign of approval. Kai rewarded her with a full smile which pleased her to no end…until Kai turned that smile on me.

Forgetting himself once more, he said, "Elyse? Did you see? Isn't it marvelous?"

At once, Miss Hawking's expression deflated.

"I think Miss Hawking is the cleverest tinker I've ever met," I said, linking my arm in hers, drawing Kai's attention to her once more.

Kai frowned a little, looking confused. He turned to her and nodded. "Indeed. It's very remarkable, Miss Hawking."

"You're very kind."

Kai pulled out his pocket watch. "I'm afraid the time is slipping away from us. I don't want you to be late," he said, turning to me.

"I have a performance this morning," I explained to Miss Hawking.

She smiled. "Then let me see you both out."

We stopped a moment in the parlor to bid Master Hawking farewell, Kai promising to return again in the evening to check on the patient.

"Father, why doesn't Doctor Murray come for dinner," Miss Hawking suggested. "And Miss McKenna too, if you are free."

"Thank you. I'm sorry I must decline. I have an engagement at that time today," Kai said.

"Miss McKenna?"

"I too must decline. I will be getting ready for a performance."

"They must have heard how terrible our cook is. Can't blame them," Master Hawking said with a smile. "Another time, another time. Come later, if you can. We'll have a spot of brandy."

Kai nodded.

I waved nicely to them, and then Kai and I headed back toward the Frost Fair.

Kai held out his arm which I took.

"You're terrible," I told him as we walked.

"Terrible?" Kai asked, sounding truly alarmed. "How so?"

"At being a bachelor."

Kai was quiet for a moment then said. "I'm afraid I miss your meaning."

"And that is the problem. I believe Miss Hawking is quite fond of you. Haven't you noticed?"

"Is she?" Kai asked, considering.

"Well?

"Well, what?"

"And you? Do you have any…attachment to her?"

Kai laughed. "Elyse. Seriously?"

"Yes, seriously."

"She is very pretty. And very clever."

"So then?"

"So then nothing."

"So, she is attractive and intelligent. And, I believe, you like and respect her father. You don't find her a good match?"

Kai was quiet. His reply was so long in coming that I was confounded.

"Kai?" I asked.

"I'm not interested in her. Now, stop playing faerie godmother. You're not on the stage yet," he said, his voice light with jest.

"Bear," I murmured.

"Faerie," he retorted, making me laugh. Suddenly, the knot that had lodged itself in my stomach untied.

7
JUST ANOTHER WHIRLWIND

WE'D HARDLY REACHED THE FIRST of the Frost Fair tents when a boy came running up to us.

"Doctor Murray?" he asked, his cheeks red, his breath forming a cloud of steam. I couldn't help but notice his heavy accent. He wore a bearskin coat and cap. Dark, curling hair escaped from under his hat. His eyes were so deep brown that they seemed almost black.

"Yes?"

"The captain," he said, pointing to one of the ships frozen in the ice. "Will you come?"

I smiled at Kai. "Well, you were right about one thing. In this weather, you'll certainly be needed here."

"I'll come see you when I can," Kai said, patting my arm.

"Titania will be ready," I replied with a grin. I waved to Kai, watching him follow the boy to the ship, then turned toward the theatre.

I walked down Freezeland Lane. The vendors were just opening their tents for the day. The smells of oil cakes and fried pork perfumed the air.

A sharp wind blew across the Thames, carrying with it a light dusting of snow. It shimmered as it blew around me like crystal dust. The strange wind so encompassed me that I stopped. The wind, shimmering in the morning sunlight, spiraled around me. The light struck the sand-fine ice so that blobs of light shimmered incandescently. I removed my glove and held out my hand, feeling the icy wind. The strange torrent slid through my fingers like silk. It pulled my hair free from its binds. Long strands of my pale blonde locks swirled around me.

A moment later, I heard a sound like the tinkling of tiny silver bells, then the wind dissipated. Once the torrent had cleared, I found myself standing across from the fine gentleman I had seen the night before. He wore a blue coat trimmed with ermine and silver buttons. His hair was pulled back at the nape, and he sported a top hat. His fair locks were very long and not of the London fashion.

He stood staring at me longer than was appropriate, but his manner was not menacing. More, he seemed transfixed. It happened from time to time, fans of the theatre forgetting that we were mere performers, after all.

"Good morning, sir. Such an odd wind, wasn't it? Did you see it?"

At this, he smiled, his blue eyes shimmering brightly. "It was a whirlwind."

"Quite magical," I said, "but I fear my hair fared the worse for it." I tried to smooth my wild locks. "I really need to carry a hand mirror."

The man smiled. "The wind only teased awake your beauty. Such a natural grace. You should let it hang long, not hide it with pins."

His flattery and frankness confirmed he was definitely not an Englishman. But aside from that, his voice held an accent that was not quite Welsh, not quite Irish, but something altogether different. I couldn't help but feel the effect of his compliment. He was certainly a gentleman and a handsome one at that. But I was also well aware of the fact that actresses had a reputation for being easily won. And if I had any hopes of making a case for myself with the Waldegraves, I needed to keep my reputation above ill-repute.

"Thank you," I said, feeling my cheeks redden.

"You are very welcome. You are, by far, the fairest maiden on the Thames, Miss McKenna."

"Sir…" I protested politely.

When he did not respond, I looked up only to see he was gone. I looked around but saw nothing but the frozen Thames. Odd manners, indeed! Shaking off the encounter, I headed toward the theatre once more.

When I arrived, I heard the voices of my troupe members in the tent backstage. Clearest of all was Marion complaining bitterly about something. Harold, one of the stagehands, was busy lighting the braziers around the benches. He looked up when I approached.

"What's Marion on about?" I asked.

He screwed up his face to show his annoyance. "Oh, she's mad that Lizzie is playing the cinder girl. Best let her get it out before you go back. Besides, an admirer has been waiting for you this half hour," he said, pointing to a figure sitting on the front bench near the brazier. John.

I nodded in thanks then hurried to him.

"Good morning," I called gaily, burying all feelings of worry.

John rose to his feet. When he turned, a look of apology crossed his handsome features. He moved to meet me.

"Miss McKenna," he said, fully aware that we were in plain sight.

"My Lord."

"Please accept my apologies. I am so sorry I was unable to stay last night," he said then held out a bundle he carried: Frost Fair roses.

"They are calling them Frost Fair roses. In Spain, they were pale purple. London's ice has turned them blue. Please, accept them with my apologies."

I took the roses from his hand. The small bundle was a petite version of Kai's gift but every bit as lovely. "Thank you," I said with a curtsey, though my heart bid me to take him into my arms.

"Just as I left you last night I was met with an urgent message. Word came that my father had taken a turn for the worse. I had to go at once. I returned later, but you were no longer here."

"Oh dear! How is your father?"

"Elys—Miss McKenna, would you care to sit near the fire. It is quite cold," he said, motioning toward the brazier.

And if we sat, we may speak more freely. Our backs to the crowd, the tent drapes sheltering us from the common eye, we'd also go unrecognized.

I nodded then we took our seats.

Once our backs were turned, he took my hand in his then reached out to touch my hair. So surprised to see him, I'd forgotten that the icy whirlwind had teased it into a wild mess.

"Oh dear," I said, lifting a hand to brush my locks back. "I got caught in the wind."

"You look very beautiful," he said. He took a lock of my pale hair between his fingers and stroked it gently. "I…I am so sorry I missed your show. You must have worried."

I nodded.

John smiled, his cheeks dimpling. He reached out and touched my chin. "Pretty lady," he said then smiled. "My father is a very proper man. We are not close, but I am his only son. My father doesn't have modern sensibilities in many matters." His meaning was plain. If there was an obstacle to our match, it was his father. "But my father is unwell. I do not expect him to last out the spring. I will inherit his title after him, then my path is my own. Elyse, I am sorry to ask this of you, but would you be willing to keep our mutual attachment quiet for a time longer until I can sort out the best course for us?"

"Of course," I said, feeling my heart beating hard in my chest.

"It's just my father…to him, our mutual fondness would be considered a scandal, and I fear my inheritance would be at stake if he knew how sincere my affections are toward you. He may do something rash. I'm sorry. This is such a serious talk so early in the morning. I just wanted to reassure you of my intent."

"John," I whispered softly. "It's all right. I understand."

He smiled, albeit sadly. "I hate the thought that you feel mistreated."

I shook my head. "Not at all. I know my heart has leaped above its station. I must follow your lead here."

John sighed heavily. "I hate that you think like that. Your heart has leaped into my hand, and for that, I am eternally grateful. You know how much I adore you," he said with a soft whisper. Looking over his shoulder, and seeing no one save Harold nearby, he leaned in and set a sweet kiss on my lips. His mouth carried the taste of anise, which seemed unusual for this hour of the day, but I fell into his kiss all the same. My heart beat hard in my chest as I felt his hand undo the button on my coat near my waist. He slipped his hand inside my coat and gently stroked my waist, his fingers grazing the bottom of my breast.

Gasping, I leaned back.

"Elyse," he groaned softly, leaning his forehead against mine.

My emotions tumbled over themselves. The deep affection I held for him was undeniable. And the stirring between my legs made me ache, but I also felt…embarrassed. Would he touch a fine lady so? Maybe I was just being silly. He touched me like that because he felt as passionate for me as I felt for him.

Not seeming to notice my confusion, he whispered, "I must apologize, but I have some business in the city today. When will you be free?"

"There is a pantomime this morning, then we break and set up for the evening performance."

"Then I will be back around noon. Wait for me?"

I nodded.

"What part will you play this morning?" he asked, gently touching my chin once more.

"Columbine fashioned as Persephone."

John clapped his hands in delight. "I will clear my schedule and be here for the show tomorrow morning." He rose. "Let me get on with my affairs so I may return by midday."

"Thank you again," I said, looking down at the Frost Fair roses.

"They are beautiful, but nowhere near as lovely as you." He put on his hat and with a soft smile, took his leave.

I lifted the roses and tried to breathe in their scent. They carried no perfume. It was as if the smell had been arrested in ice.

I sighed.

Lady Waldegrave.

That was certainly a title worth waiting for.

8

OF POMEGRANATES,
OIL CAKES, AND BITTER CHOCOLATE

AS I APPROACHED THE TENT backstage, I heard Marion's high-pitched tone matched in passion with Lizzie's angry voice. Lizzie, from what I could tell, was beyond frustrated. When I rounded the corner, I found Marve standing between Lizzie and Marion while Hobbs, who would play Hades to my Persephone, stood in the background listening.

"You've given Lizzie and Elyse the best parts in *Midwinter*. And now in the pantomime too. Given my years with the company, and my far superior talent to any actress in this troupe, it's unfair," Marion said.

Her dark eyes flicked toward me. I could see her calculating, determining if I had heard her last comment. Deciding that I had, she smirked. "At least you could have given me Persephone," she added then glared at me.

Marve sighed then following Marion's gaze.

"What's the matter?" I asked.

Lizzie, Marion, and Marve all spoke at once. And of course, it was the expected argument.

The truth of the matter was that Marion was a very good actress. She was better than Amy and Hannah who were still more enthusiastic than talented. But she was not better than Lizzie. And she was not better than me. She was also the oldest woman in our company, and her roles reflected that.

Marve raised his hands. "You know Elyse gets all the dancing parts. She is the only trained ballerina in our troupe."

"Trained by her grandmother, which hardly counts," Marion protested.

"My grandmother was a ballerina for—" I began in protest but was cut off.

"We are at the Frost Fair but a week, maybe not even that long, before the Thames takes the river back. Can't you, not even for one performance, give me a lead role?" Marion demanded angrily. But this time, I saw a flash behind her eyes. Certainly, she was jealous. But it was more than that. She truly found it unfair. And maybe it was. I might be a better dancer, and our presence on the stage was very different, but she was a very good actress.

I opened my mouth to offer her the role of Persephone, but the words stuck in my throat. Hobbs, seeing me move to speak, shook his head. Offering it would have been the right, the generous, thing to do. But somehow, I couldn't bring myself to give up the role. My chances to do ballet on stage were so few, and if managers for the other stages were at the fair, it would be my chance to shine. Ever since I stepped foot on stage, I had wanted to act for one of the big houses. Being part of a troupe at a more reputable house made me a more reputable woman, which was something I needed more than anything at the moment.

Marion slammed down the faerie godmother's wand then turned and headed deeper into the tent. "Ridiculous. All of you are ridiculous, talentless hacks. I have half a mind to quit!"

Marve sighed heavily then pinched his brow.

"You were right not to give in," Hobbs told him. "If you give in now, she'll try to pressure you every time."

"She's terribly good at drama, but all we are staging is comedy," Lizzie said.

Marion played the darker ladies like Gertrude, Lady MacBeth, and the Duchess of Malfi. Drama was her specialty. But for the fair, Marve had planned only comedies to keep things light. Lizzie was right.

Marve sighed once more. And this time, that sigh was pregnant with unspoken words. He turned and looked at me.

"Elyse," he began gently. "Marion cannot play the cinder girl. She is too old. But she has studied as Columbine and can play Persephone. Maybe, just this once, on account of the fair..."

"Marve," Hobbs exclaimed. "She doesn't dance anywhere near as well as Elyse, and her timing for humor is off."

"True. But, as she said, we'll be back to our playhouse in a week. And Elyse knows the faerie godmother lines. As well, you can wear Titania's costume for the part. I'd rather return with a sullen and snobbish actress rather than have her leave our company."

I steeled myself against the frustration and jealousy that splashed up inside me. I strongly suspected that I was feeling exactly how Marion felt. "I can do what's best for our troupe."

"This is poorly done," Hobbs told Marve.

"Maybe," he said. "But it must be done. Thank you, Elyse."

I nodded then sat down on a barrel and started to pull my hair back into a braid while Marve went to find Marion.

Hobbs shook his head in frustration then headed back to his section to get ready.

"We don't go on until after their set, and I've been smelling oil cakes all morning. Join me, faerie godmother?" Lizzie asked, extending her hand.

I nodded. "After I get my hair in place."

"Are those more Frost Fair roses?" she asked, looking at the bundle in my hand.

I grinned.

"Would I get wooed as often as you. Your gentleman caller...I saw him waiting for you in the front. Handsome rake."

"Rake! Oh no. He is quite sincere, I assure you."

Lizzie lifted an eyebrow at me. The expression was charming. I remembered her using it on stage before. "Are you—please forgive me for asking—but are you certain? You know how some gentlemen look at us—"

"Very certain."

"Oh!" Lizzie exclaimed, her other eyebrow joining the first in surprise. "Oh, that is good news. But what about Doctor Murray?"

"What about him?"

"I just thought…"

"Heavens, no. He is like my brother."

Lizzie pursed her lips. "Well, if that's the case."

I laughed. "He's far too sullen for you."

She grinned. "I expected as much. What happened to your hair, anyway?"

"A wind snarled it. Do you remember a gentleman at the show last night? You might have marked him. He wore a blue suit and coat. His hair was very pale blond, long, and not in the London fashion. He was very handsome."

Lizzie shook her head. "No. I don't. But from the sound of it, I'm sorry I missed him."

"Perhaps he'll be back today." Odd. Lizzie always noticed the handsome attendees, which was, no doubt, how Kai had gotten her attention. Surly though he was, women always found his dark hair and hazel eyes very appealing.

I finished tying off my braid then nodded to Lizzie that I was ready to go just as Marion appeared. Paying no attention to us, she was smiling at the ground. When she realized we were there, she quickly made her expression blank.

"Have you been informed?" she asked, a smug look on her face.

Informed? As if I had not acquiesced. Informed, indeed!

Her cheeks flushing red with anger, Lizzie opened her mouth to speak, but I took her arm and squeezed it gently.

"Yes, I have. You'll find Persephone's costume in my trunk."

Marion nodded, gave me a half-snort, then turned and walked toward my section.

"Whey-faced adder," Lizzie grumbled in her direction.

I elbowed her gently in the ribs. "Forget her. Let's go."

Lizzie and I turned back toward Freezeland Lane and headed out in the direction of the oil cake vendor. The thoroughfare was getting very crowded as even more Londoners joined the revelry on the ice. The scent of oil cakes perfumed the chilly air. We approached the vendor.

"Ladies," the vendor called happily. "How many?"

"One for each of us," Lizzie said.

"Shall I add some snow?" he asked, motioning to some powdered sugar.

At the mention of the sugar, I was reminded of the gentleman who'd fallen into the ice. I'd have to stop by and check on him later that day. I'm sure Kai would not be opposed to visiting the Hawkings' workshop once more.

"Oh, please," Lizzie replied, eyeing the cake hungrily.

Trading coins for the cakes, we moved back into the gathering crowd.

"There is a tent two rows over where they are selling handbills to commemorate the fair. Let's get one," Lizzie said, directing me once more.

Though it was still morning, the crowd was already beginning to pick up. Slender rays of sunlight shone down on the Thames. If it warmed up, the fair would be over before it started. This, of course, was good news to all the sailors trapped in the ice. But my troupe, and many other vendors, were set to make a fat stack of coins from the impromptu festivities.

A small crowd gathered around a painter who had set up his easel and was painting one of the ships trapped in the ice. We passed vendor tents where frozen meats, fish, and other goods were for sale. One baker sold gingerbread. The scents of the baking bread, cinnamon, anise, and other spices wafted through the air. Children laughed loudly as a man swung them on a massive swing built from tall timbers frozen into the ice, the swing made from a sleigh. Four children sat laughing, their cheeks red, as those around cheered and waved to them as they swung. Not far from them, the usual debauchery also found its home at The Frozen Mushroom. I caught the scent of opium on the wind and noticed people sipping gin.

The first day of the Frost Fair had seen mostly commoners on the ice. Now, however, I noted more fine ladies and gentlemen in the crowd. Perhaps this was why Marion was so insistent on having a larger role. She knew the audience would be of a better sort today. This also meant that at tonight's performance I would have to play Titania with renewed vigor. I was suddenly sorry I'd let Marion take the role of Persephone. I rarely had a chance to show off my skills in ballet, and Marve had written the script for me for that express purpose. Tomorrow, I would insist on having my role back.

We approached the other end of the Frost Fair. The fair, situated on the ice between London and Blackfriars Bridges, thinned out near the Blackfriars end where the ice was said to be thinnest.

"There," Lizzie said, pointing to a line of people waiting to get a handbill.

"Get one for me? I'll get us both a hot chocolate," I said, pointing to another vendor across the lane.

I joined the long queue of people waiting to get a cup of steaming chocolate. The copper kettle from which the vendor was ladling the drink effervesced the sweetest perfume. The scent of cocoa filled the air. The delicious aroma fought off the smells coming from a makeshift tavern and gaming tent nearby. Someone had written *City of Moscow* on a board and had hung it over the entrance. The smells of ale and smoke billowed from the tent.

I looked back at Lizzie, who was chatting with two young women in line behind her.

I finished off the last bite of oil cake then clapped my hands, freeing them of the loose sugar, as I waited. Once more, a strong wind whipped across the ice. The tents' walls, many of which had been made from sails, snapped and shifted in the hard breeze.

I pulled up my hood, afraid the wind would take my hair apart once more. Holding my cape shut at the neck, I turned from the wind and found myself facing the City of Moscow tent. The wind blew insistently around me, and with my other hand, I held down the skirts of my dress to fight off the unexpected updraft. The sharp wind pulled a peg from the ground, and one corner of the tent at the City of Moscow pulled free, revealing the revelers inside.

"Next," the gentleman at the hot chocolate stand called.

With the tent flap pulled aside, I looked into the City of Moscow and spotted several gentlemen sitting at a makeshift gaming table, all of them drinking. And for a brief moment, I swore I saw John. He tipped his head back and laughed loudly. What was he doing here? Hadn't he said he had some business in town?

"Next! You, Miss. In the blue coat."

I turned to see it was my turn.

"Sorry. Two, please," I told the man, opening my bag to retrieve my coins.

I set the coins on the table then looked back at the gaming tent. A worker had come to fix the tent flap, obscuring my view.

Turning back, I took the steaming cups of dark chocolate from the vendor. "Thank you," I said with a polite smile. The dark liquid, almost black in color, looked as thick as mud.

"I got them!" Lizzie called, crossing the ice toward me.

I handed her a drink.

"I put them in my bag so the wind didn't take them. Such an odd wind, wasn't it? My dress blew up, almost showed a glimpse of my knickers. No wonder your hair came undone. Elyse? What's wrong?"

"Can you hold this a moment?" I asked, handing her my drink.

Confused, she nodded.

I went to the entrance of the City of Moscow and looked toward the table where I thought I'd seen John. Another man sat in his place wearing a coat that was the same deep green color. The man also had the same sandy-colored hair.

"Miss?" a man said, meeting me at the entrance.

"Is...is Lord Waldegrave within?"

The man scrunched up his face and thought back. "Lord Waldegrave? No. Haven't seen him since last night."

"Last night?"

The man shrugged. "He was by for a few drinks."

Well, that was to be expected. It was a Frost Fair, after all. If he was partial to drink, that explained the taste of anise on his tongue: absinthe.

"But not this morning?"

"No, Miss."

"Very well. Thank you," I said.

I'd been mistaken. I chided myself for my distrust. What was I doing acting so suspicious? I turned and rejoined Lizzie.

"Everything all right?" she asked, handing me the cup of hot chocolate.

I nodded. "It was nothing. How is it?" I asked, motioning to the drink. "Ambrosia!" she exclaimed.

Taking her word for it, I took a sip. She was right. The drink had been brewed thick, and it carried a hint of spice. It was an unusual but well-matched flavor.

"Should we head back?" Lizzie asked.

I nodded, and we turned back toward the Ice House. As we walked, Lizzie chatted happily, pointing out all the sights. My mind, however, was busy. What kind of woman was I to doubt my love at the first opportunity? Not a very true one. I had no reason to doubt John. He'd been nothing but forthcoming with me. I sighed. It had been an odd morning. As we passed the row where Kai and I had been met by the boy that morning, I paused.

"Why don't you go ahead? I want to check on Doctor Murray."

Lizzie raised one eyebrow at me again. "Do you want me to come with you?"

"No, I'll be fine. Kai—Doctor Murray went to check on a patient. I just thought I'd see if he needs anything."

Lizzie smirked but said nothing. "Don't be long."

With a wave, I turned and headed across the ice toward the ship where the boy had led Kai. My nerves were rattled. Had I really seen John? I wasn't sure. What I did know, however, was that nothing comforted me more than Kai's advice and opinion. I knew that spending just a moment or two with Kai would make everything right again.

9
THE CAPTAIN

OUTSIDE THE SHIP, A SMALL area of the ice had been swept of snow. I wasn't sure how they'd done it, but the ice appeared to have been washed. Its surface was an oval of glass upon which some of the sailors were skating. Their moves were sublime. They skated with such ease, moving around each other in a pattern that reminded me of a quadrille. Nearby, someone had carved a lovely castle made of ice. It seemed the sailors had decided to make their ship as festive as possible. Lanterns sat along the rail, and from inside the galley, I heard music.

I approached carefully. I looked over the skaters and the other merry-makers but didn't see Kai. A moment later, the boy who'd asked Kai to come with him appeared on deck. He grabbed a rope and slid down to the surface of the frozen Thames then ran over to me.

"Miss?"

"I was looking for Doctor Murray. Is he still here?"

The boy scrunched up his brow as if he was not sure what to say. "Yes. He is still with the captain."

"May I see him? I just wanted a word." A word. A comfort. A reassurance. A...something.

The boy thought over my request for longer than seemed needed. "Certainly," he said. He smiled then, both cheeks dimpling in a mischievous grin. Waving to me, he beckoned me to follow him.

The skaters slowed as I approached. I noticed that, like the boy, many of them had long dark hair which they let hang loose down their backs. They were a very attractive group of men. The leatherworking on their attire was remarkable. Where were they from? They nodded to me then went back about their business.

"This way, Miss," the boy said.

I walked up a plank onto the deck of the ship. There, several of the sailors sat around a brazier while they played unusual instruments: long-necked lutes, oddly-shaped harps, and one man even played what appeared to be a flute made of...ice? I stopped when I saw it.

"Is that...Is that made of ice?" I asked, unable to stop myself.

The boy smiled. "Indeed."

"But how?"

"Magic, of course," the boy replied with a wink then waved for me to follow him to the captain's quarters. When he reached the door, he knocked.

At first, there was no answer. I heard muffled voices and movement inside. I frowned, conscious that time was passing quickly. I needed to get back soon. Maybe I should have come later.

The boy knocked again. "Captain? Doctor Murray's friend is here."

The voices on the other side of the door fell silent.

A moment later, a man in a wolf pelt coat opened the door. He gave me a hard look which unnerved me. I looked around him hoping to catch sight of Kai. I spotted Kai's boots.

"Doctor Murray?" I called.

The man at the door frowned then stepped aside to let me in.

The cabin within was nothing like what I expected. Rather than finding a captain's lodging complete with a table, desk, or rough cot, the room was very finely appointed with rich furniture. Colorful tapestries hung on the walls and bear furs covered the floor. The furniture appeared to have been made by artisans with great craft, each piece adorned with figures and old Celtic knots. Even the moulding around the ceiling had been carved to look like a line of leaves. The room was warm and softly perfumed like lavender. In the midst of this unexpected scene was Kai, who was wrapping a bandage around a strikingly beautiful woman's ankle. The woman, I realized, was staring at me. She had long, curly dark hair, wide dark eyes, and red lips. Her face was very pale and so perfect she looked like she'd been carved of marble. She wore a green gown trimmed with ermine. She'd pulled up her dress to her knee, a scandalous amount of leg exposed.

"Doctor Murray?" I said again, calling to Kai who still, or so it seemed, had not noticed me.

"Doctor, your friend is here," the woman said then smirked. The strange expression on her face froze my heart. Her look was full of so much unexpected malice it surprised me.

Kai stopped and looked up at me. "Miss McKenna? What are you doing here?"

The sharpness of his question confused me. "I thought...I wondered...I just wanted to see if you need anything. Can I can assist you?"

Kai frowned in confusion, his forehead furrowing.

"Doctor Murray has been very good to me. You see," the woman said, waving to her ankle. "I twisted my ankle while skating."

"Oh, I thought the boy said the captain was injured," I replied, realizing then that no one had introduced me to the woman.

"I am the captain," she replied.

I choked down a gasp. "My apologies, Captain. Are you...are you well now?"

The woman huffed then suppressed a sneer. "So, you are the actress everyone is talking about. The girl who plays at being the faerie queen."

The man in the wolf pelt chuckled.

"I'm Miss Elyse McKenna," I said, looking toward Kai. Why was he being so rude? I hated when Kai was so focused on his work that he forgot his manners. "I'm an actress at the Ice House Theatre. We normally perform at Struthers Theatre but have come for the Frost Fair."

"You don't look like I thought you would," she said then rolled her eyes toward her companion. "He oversold her a bit, I think."

The man sniggered.

Having had enough of the captain who clearly had the manners of a pirate, I turned to Kai. "Doctor Murray, do you need any assistance or are you finished here?"

Kai paused then looked up at me. "Elyse? What? No...no...I think I'm almost done," he said, looking confused.

"Excellent. Then I'll see you at this morning's show." I ladened my voice with unspoken words, hoping Kai would take the hint that he really ought to get out of there, but he didn't look back.

I bobbed a curtsey to the captain. "I wish you a speedy recovery, Captain," I said. "And I hope that the ice melts soon."

"That, at least, is something I can agree upon."

I curtseyed again then turned to exit.

The gentleman in wolf furs held the door for me.

Without another word, I left.

Outside, the little boy sat on the deck of the ship listening to the musicians. The ice flute produced such an unusual sounding reel. The music had such a lovely sound and vibration to it. It was enchanting.

Despite the sour mood that had settled over me, the beautiful music was delightful. When the boy spotted me, he stood up.

"This way, Miss. Careful on the plank. The ice is slippery," he said. Taking me gently by the elbow, he led me across the deck of the ship and down the plank.

The skaters still spun as we passed. The boy walked me back to the lane closest to the tents.

"Thank you," I said, smiling down at him. "I'm sorry, I didn't catch your name."

"Robin."

"Robin. Thank you, Robin. And your captain...I'm afraid Doctor Murray was so busy he forgot his manners. I was unable to learn your captain's name."

"Captain Behra."

"Captain Behra," I repeated. "Very good. Thank you, Robin."

"Miss," he said with a bow then turned and headed back toward the ship.

Frustrated, and feeling more ill-at-ease than ever, I headed back toward the theatre. At least there, I knew my place. At least there, I knew who I was. I was no one and everyone. And right now, getting lost to who I was sounded like a very good thing.

10
A SORTA FAIRYTALE

WHEN I ARRIVED AT THE Ice House Theatre, the patrons were already being seated for the pantomime of Hades and Persephone. I passed Marion as I headed toward my section of the large tent behind our makeshift stage. She was dressed in my Persephone costume, looking like the perfect image of spring, silk flowers in her hair, wearing a belt of ivy. She carried a pair of dancing slippers, *my* dancing slippers.

"Marion...those are not part of the costume. They actually belong to me. They were a gift."

She looked down at the slippers. I could see the wash of confusion then frustration pass over her face. "These old things? I almost left them, ragged as they are. I thought Marve had assigned them for the costume. I don't care about your precious slippers, Elyse."

I bit the inside of my cheek then said. "It's just that they were—"

"A gift. I heard you. I have my own slippers anyway, and not old rags like these," she said, practically tossing the ballet shoes to me. She turned toward her own section of the tent.

I clutched my pale pink ballet slippers. She was right. They were old and ragged, but they were also a gift from my grandmother. She'd bought me the pair when I'd joined the company five years back.

I hugged the slippers to my chest then went to my station and sat down. The tent was heated by braziers, the floor strewn with hay for warmth. Partitions offered a little privacy. I slipped off my cloak, shivering in the cold, then began working on my hair. For the faerie godmother, I would pull it up in a bun to create a different effect from Titania, who wore long, loose locks trimmed with feathers, flowers, and sparkles. I wouldn't use the glimmer cream either. Instead, I'd seek to look more matronly.

As I worked my hair, I heard the sound of trumpets and flutes marking the beginning of the show. My heartbeat quickened, and once more I felt deeply annoyed with Marion. With so many important people on the ice this morning, she'd stolen my chance.

For the good of the troupe.

For the good of the troupe.

I reminded myself over and over again.

THE PANTOMIME OF HADES AND Persephone finished within an hour. By the time it was done, I had transformed myself once again into a faerie. Rather than Titania, I was the benevolent faerie godmother ready to bestow gifts on the sweet cinder maid.

I heard the applause from the crowd. The performance had been well-received, and from the sound of it, the crowd was quite large.

It would take a few moments to change the set.

Giving my hair one last look, I grabbed the faerie godmother's wand and headed out of the tent to the backstage area.

Lizzie, dressed as the cinder girl, Amy as one of the stepsisters, Hannah as a second stepsister, and Agnes as the stepmother, prepared to take the stage alongside Robert, who would play the father who perished in act one, leaving Lizzie to the cruel care of her stepmother.

"Elyse, you look lovely," Lizzie said, smiling at me. "Is that really the same costume?"

I nodded. "I removed the wings, and added a shawl," I said, motioning to the soft pink wrap.

"Marion tripped…twice," she whispered, leaning toward me.

"They made it look like part of the act," Amy added, clearly clued into the gossip.

I forced myself not to smile then chided myself for my pettiness. "How is the crowd?" I asked, winking knowingly to Lizzie as I changed the subject.

"Elyse, you're too good," Hannah said with a giggle.

"Not really. I'm just trying to be good," I replied.

The girls chuckled.

"The crowd is bigger than last night," Robert said. "It's…there are a lot of lords and ladies in attendance."

This made Lizzie and Amy go silent.

"No matter, girls," Agnes said. "We'll do our best no matter the manner of the crowd."

"But they…these fine folk usually go to the big theatres. They'll be expecting…" Amy began but trailed off.

"We are all very fine actors," I said reassuringly. "Simply because we didn't have connections to get us into a grand playhouse does not mean we lack in skill. All of us are masters at our craft. We know our work. We will, as always, transport them," I said, sounding more confident than I felt. In reality, I had never even practiced the role of the faerie godmother. I knew the lines, and I'd seen the marks, but had not practiced them. My stomach quaked.

Lizzie, Amy, and Hannah looked reassured. Robert and Agnes nodded to me.

Flutes sounded once more, and the others headed out on stage.

Robert went to the front and began to address the audience as the prologue.

"In a fine chateau lived a gentleman of means with a loving wife and a fair daughter who was a mirror reflection of her mother. Tragically, the young wife died, but the gentleman—that is me—found a new love. Upon his marriage, he returned once more to his country estate to introduce his new wife, and her daughters, to his blessed child. The rest, as they say…" he said, and here I knew he would flourish his arm toward the stage behind him as a harp sounded in time. The curtain drew back to reveal the actresses.

"My dear family," Robert said. I caught just a glimpse of him as he passed across the stage holding a letter. "My travel is set. I am to leave on the 'morrow. What can I bring you all upon my return?"

"Jewels!" Hannah shouted.

"Silk, gowns, ribbons," Amy shouted.

"A hat of the new fashion," Agnes added.

Robert laughed. "Girls, girls, I shall endeavor to do my best. But what of my Ella? What would you like, my dear?"

"Bring me…bring me the first branch that touches your hat on your way home to me," Lizzie said with such earnest sweetness that I raised my eyebrows. She was playing her best that morning.

At that, the other actresses laughed meanly. Marion had certainly missed her calling, I thought then turned and looked through a crack in the wood at the audience. I scanned over the benches which were crowded with fine lords and ladies. They watched attentively, lost in one of their favorite tales. I looked for a familiar green coat in the crowd. Finally, I spotted him. John stood toward the rear of the audience with two other young men who looked familiar. I smiled when I saw him, my heart quickening. Oh no! He'd come to see my Persephone but found Marion instead.

I bit my bottom lip then looked for Kai. He was not beside the brazier where he'd been standing last night. In fact, I didn't see him anywhere. His manner had been so odd. Was the injury worse than it looked? Maybe he was so fixed on setting her ankle to right that he'd forgotten himself. It wasn't unusual for him to be distracted with a patient, but it was unusual for him to be rude. Had Kai ever been rude to me before? I couldn't remember a time.

Robert passed me as he left the stage, and the harp fluttered as the scene changed.

"Dead already?" I whispered.

Robert nodded. "Now to get a pint or two before faerie time," he said with a wink then left.

I watched John as he stood with his fellows. They spoke in low tones, smiling and jostling one another. Who were these other young gentlemen? They seemed quite…jovial. Were they simply merry or were they intoxicated? I scanned the crowd once more. My eyes stopped, however, when I spotted the fine foreign gentleman. He stood in the middle of the crowd, seemingly unaware of the crush of people around him. Both of his hands rested on his walking stick in front of him as he watched the tale unfold.

I smiled. He really was very handsome. His features were fine, not a hint of a beard on him, his lips curving perfectly.

Even as I thought it, the gentleman's gaze shifted. He turned and looked at me. He smiled.

Gasping, I leaned back from the open cranny in the slab.

"*Cinder*wench!"

"*Cinder*ella!"

I turned back toward the stage and watched as the tragedy unfolded. Her father lost, left to the devices of her stepmother, Ella's life began to crumble. The play moved forward, and finally, fate had bruised Cinderella enough.

Alone on stage, Lizzie wept with her head in her arms before a mock fireplace. "Oh, mother. Oh, father. Oh, wicked fate," she wailed.

Holding my wand, I moved nimbly, floating onto the stage with a dancer's grace. Skippy strummed the harp lightly, a tinkling of sound enchanting the space.

The audience held its breath.

Moving carefully, I let myself dissolve into the character. I let myself feel the godmother's concern, love, and pity for the sweet maiden. I also felt a little sting of anger, wanting to take revenge on the jealous stepmother and sisters.

"Like an airy spirit, I

Granting wishes as I pass by

How now, sweet young thing

A face far fairer than the spring

Do not weep, do not cry

Let me, your faerie godmother, dry thy eye."

"Did you say...did you say *faerie* godmother?" Lizzie, as Ella, asked with a sniff. She sat up and looked at me, wiping real tears from her eyes. *Impressive.*

I smiled nicely and curtseyed to her.

"Do not despair, my precious dear.

Your faerie godmother is now here

And to the ball, you'll swiftly go

A maiden more of joy than woe."

And on we went. A pumpkin, four stuffed mice, two clay lizards, a gown, and a pair of glittery shoes later, my scene ended, and Lizzie was off to the ball.

As I made my exit, I heard a whistle from the back of the crowd. I looked back to see John smiling and clapping for me. His chaps grinned from him to me.

I cast my eyes across the audience once more.

Kai had not come.

The foreign gentleman, however, inclined his head to me.

Blushing, I headed backstage to wait until the final curtain call.

"Well done," Marve whispered. "And don't worry. We'll have you back as Persephone tomorrow. Marion was a disaster."

Behind us, someone cleared their throat.

It was Marion.

"Ah, Marion," Marve said, a guilty look crossing his face.

"I wanted to talk to you about my costume in *Midwinter*'s wedding scene," she said, frowning. It was clear she heard but was pretending she had not.

Marve nodded to me then headed to the backstage tent with Marion.

I smiled as I watched Lizzie in the ballroom scene. Her dazzling blue and gold ball gown shimmered in the morning sunlight. Her curls, twisted into ringlets, bounced nicely as she and her prince danced.

I peered out at the audience through the crack in the wood once more. The ladies' eyes sparkled with delight as they saw the cinder girl win her prince at the ball. Alas, when the clock struck twelve, Cinderella had to flee, her slipper left behind.

James, playing the role of the prince, searched desperately for the girl with the glass slipper. The ladies in the audience winced, hiding their faces in their fur muffs as the stepsisters sliced off their toes to try to fit their feet into the dainty slipper. One lady swooned when Amy took a knife to her toes, dropping a red handkerchief filled with wooden toes onto the stage. Despite Amy's and Hannah's best efforts, they could not fit the shoe that I had created just for the cinder girl.

"Perhaps I can try," Lizzie said demurely.

Hannah and Amy laughed.

James slid the slipper on Lizzie's dainty foot.

"A perfect fit," he said with a gasp.

At that, Lizzie slid on her second slipper and was led off stage, leaving Hannah and Amy to weep. Lizzie quickly stripped off the cinder girl's humble frock and slid on a wedding gown. I hurriedly laced the back while Agnes tidied her hair and set a ring of flowers on her head.

The others exited the other side of the stage, and soon the wedding march sounded. Remodeled into a bride, Lizzie and James joined hands and took the stage. With a few sweet words and kisses, the play ended.

It had gone well, but I was very glad it was done. I spied out the crack once more. John and his companions were gone. Perhaps he was waiting at the back? My heart beat a little harder. Surely he would not leave again. I scanned around for Kai. Neither he nor the foreign gentleman were anywhere to be seen.

Suddenly, I was all out of suitors.

I chuckled, chiding myself. Kai was, most certainly, not a suitor.

And the foreign gentleman? Well, maybe next time it wouldn't hurt to ask his name.

Once the story concluded, we waited for a final curtain call. Then, at last, we would break until the evening's performance. I'd have a whole day to spend with John, assuming he hadn't run into any emergency errands again. But even as I thought it, I knew I was being unfair. After all, his father was ill. But if his father was ill, why was he in London rather than at their home in Twickenham? I frowned.

Gathering together, we took the stage once more to cheers and calls of bravo. It seemed to me that the crowd, merry from their enjoyment of being at the fair, was far more enthusiastic than the simple play warranted. But, all the same, they seemed to be pleased with the performance. And in truth, Lizzie had played her part very well.

At last, they let us go.

"Well done," I cheered Lizzie, linking my arm in hers.

"I think it went over well. I felt the character—as you are always telling me to try to—and it did change my performance, I think."

"You did wonderfully," Agnes told her with a smile.

"Nice work, Lizzie," Marve told her.

"Sir, Miss Lizzie," Harold said, approaching Marve and Lizzie. He handed Lizzie a copy of the playbill on which I saw some handwriting.

Lizzie took it from him. Her hand trembling, she read: "For the cinder girl. Very notably enacted. I invite you to call on me. Master James Grady, Sadler's Wells Theatre."

Everyone went silent.

When Lizzie looked up, her eyes were wet with tears.

"Oh, Lizzie," I whispered. "Sadler's Wells! That's…remarkable," I said then pulled her into an embrace.

The others soon wrapped their arms around her as well and all at once, we fell into a crushing hug, everyone giggling and laughing, Lizzie in tears at the center.

When we finally let her go, Marve cleared his throat. "I'm making buckets of money at this fair, but it hardly seems worth the expense of losing a wonderful actress."

"Well, I'm not lost yet," Lizzie said.

"Dear girl, we all know what a note like that means. Call on him tomorrow morning. Amy can play the role of Cinderella for you. We'll have Skippy play the other sister," Marve said.

I laughed. Skippy, our young errand boy, would not be in a good mood after learning this news.

"Come on. Let's go celebrate. Elyse?" Amy said.

"Sorry. I'm meeting someone."

"Elyse and her gentleman," Lizzie said with a roll of the eyes, teasing me.

I smiled at her.

"Let's go," she said to the other girls and they headed to the tent, leaving Marve and me alone.

"I'm sorry, Elyse," Marve said.

"Sorry? Whatever for?"

"Marion...if you had played Persephone this morning, there would have been two notes. The faerie godmother was well-played, but it's such a small, trifling part."

"If I was the suspicious type, I'd say you sabotaged me on purpose," I jested.

Marve went pale. "Elyse, I'd never—"

I grinned then kissed him on the cheek. "I know, I know. Granny used to say there was no more honest man of the stage in London than you."

Marve wrapped his arm around me then, patting me on the back.

"Now, let me see about my gentleman." With a wave, I headed toward my small dressing area. On the other side of the tent, I heard the girls gushing loudly, all excited for Lizzie's great news. I pulled my hair out of its bun. Sighing, I rested my elbows on my knees, my forehead on my hands. I was a fool to chase love when what I should have been chasing was my career. I should never have let Marion take my part. I was too nice, and it had cost me. Tomorrow, I would not be so nice. And if John was not waiting for me at the front of the Ice House, I didn't know what I was going to do.

I looked back into the mirror and rearranged my hair once more. I then took my ballet slippers, which I had left sitting on my trunk, and placed them back inside with the rest of my costumes. I noticed then that the Persephone costume had not been returned. I slipped out of my costume, laying it in the trunk, then pulled back on my winter gown and blue coat.

If John was not there, I'd go find Kai. I had to tell him about what had happened with Marion and Lizzie. If anyone could advise me, it was him.

I headed out of the tent toward the entrance of the Ice House Theatre. There I found a carriage waiting. A black horse, its mane decorated with bells, exhaled deeply, creating huge clouds of steam. John was sitting in the driver's seat.

I smiled when I saw him.

Slipping out of his seat, he offered me his hand.

"Come, faerie godmother, and grant me three wishes."

"I am a faerie, not a genie," I replied, placing my hand in his.

He laughed. "Then grant me just one wish," he said, stepping close.

"And what might that be?" I asked.

"A kiss," he whispered.

Hidden behind the steed, I leaned toward him. John lowered his lips onto mine. They were warm. A heady scent of sherry clung to him. I leaned into his kiss, tasting the sharp herbal and salty flavors in his mouth.

When we broke apart, my heart was beating hard. "Let's go," he said, helping me into the carriage.

"Go where?" I asked.

"And ruin the surprise? Never," he replied with a laugh.

I joined him on the seat of the carriage. He pulled a blanket over our legs, and with a click to his horse, he turned the carriage away from the Frost Fair toward the city. Under the cover of the blanket, I set my hand on his knee. John grinned, and we headed off on an adventure.

11
FOOLING MOTHER NATURE

"WHERE ARE WE GOING?" I asked with a laugh as we headed away from the frozen Thames and back into the city.

"It's a surprise," John replied.

I held my hood and looked back toward Captain Behra's frozen ship. I bit my lower lip.

The carriage rolled off the Thames and onto the cobblestone London street. A gust blew up from behind us, the wind whipping angrily off the Thames. Angry snowflakes swirled around us then died down as we made our first turn into the city.

"Strange weather on the Thames this morning," I said.

"How so?" John asked.

"The wind...one would think it has a mind of its own. It seems to whip with such purpose."

John grinned. "You have a very healthy imagination, Miss McKenna. Perhaps that's how you play so well."

I smiled. "I do try to take on the emotions of my characters, to feel what they feel."

He looked at me, an odd expression on his face. "You deceive with great craft."

"What can I say, I am an artisan," I said with exaggerated drama.

John laughed.

I snuggled closer to him as we turned through the London streets. At that moment, I hardly cared where we were headed. I loved that we were close to one another, that I felt the warmth of his body. All my worries melted away. Lizzie's warning, while well-intended, had stirred my worries and had my imagination going at the City of Moscow that morning. But as I leaned into John, all those fears disappeared.

We were getting quite close to Buckingham Palace when John turned the carriage on a side road. Unfamiliar with this part of town, I had no idea where we were headed. What I could discern, however, was that we were driving down a path through a very elaborate garden. A moment later, I spied a metal and glass roof. The white metal frame of the building was interspersed with panes of glass that glinted in the sunlight. The place was shaped like a series of domes.

"Oh my," I exclaimed, placing my fingers against my lips. "What is this place?"

"Rose House," John said with a smile. "The only warm place left in London," he added with a laugh.

"It's a herbarium?"

He nodded. "You will see. Rose House is no false moniker."

"To whom does it belong?"

"The crown, of course."

"But John…" I started, thinking to ask how in the world he would manage entry into such a place but stopped my words short. A gentleman would know such ways. An artisan would not.

He pulled the carriage to a stop outside the elaborate greenhouse. The carriage drive circled around a fountain. At its center, a marble lord and lady danced, their garlands of flowers made of stone. Ice clung to their arms and faces, and their heads were covered in inches of snow.

John slid out of the carriage then took my hand and helped me out. Given its appeal on such a cold day, I was surprised to see there were no other visitors. The path had not been cleared. Only a single set of footprints heading inside marred the snowy ground.

I stepped lightly through the snow, John holding my hand, as we went to the door. John rapped lightly on the door then called a "hello?"

A moment later, an old man wearing a heavy coat came to the door. He was the gruff sort, his face squinting with annoyance at everything he saw.

"You got it?" he asked John from the other side of the door, not bothering to even respond with the appropriate courtesy.

John nodded then lifted a small packet to show the man. "And your touring fee," John added.

The old man raised an eyebrow at him then looked at me. He snorted then turned and unlocked the door.

John handed him the package and some coin.

"You have an hour. No more," the old man told him.

John nodded, took my hand, and then led me inside.

"How very discourteous," I whispered. I tried to think of a way to ask what was in the package, but finding none, I let the matter lie.

John shrugged. "Age wears courtesy to the bone."

We passed from the outer chamber through the second set of doors into the herbarium. All at once, I was overcome with warmth and the moist air of summer. The smell of roses, water, grass, and sunshine on green leaves perfumed the space.

I gasped. "It is summer captured in glass." A butterfly passed by. I reached out, beckoning it to come to me, but it fluttered away.

John smiled and removed his top hat and gloves, setting them on a bench just inside the door. "You have such a lovely mind. Others might say 'it's so charming' whereas you find summer trapped in glass."

I giggled. "I almost said I felt trapped in a terrarium," I said as I pushed my hood back and pulled off my gloves. "But I thought that might sound strange."

He chuckled. "May I take your coat?"

I nodded then undid the fastens. I handed it to him. He draped the garment over his arm then motioned for me to follow.

"I enjoyed your faerie godmother," he told me as we made our way down the twisting path through the green. Palm trees and other wide leafy greens grew all around. "Were you not to play Persephone as well?"

I nodded. "There was some…conversation," I said, unsure how much squabbling amongst actors he'd want to hear, "and we decided that Marion would take the role for today."

"Conversation? I take that to mean argument."

"Marion was upset."

"So she stole your role."

"For a day."

John looked thoughtful. "You're too kind, Elyse."

I didn't reply. I might have given Marion the role, but I hadn't wanted to and was completely vexed about the whole thing. That didn't feel very kind to me.

"Look," John said then, pointing to a path that led through an arbor of roses. The red blossoms perfumed the air around us. From somewhere inside the herbarium, a bird chirped happily.

"It sounds like someone has found somewhere warm to shelter this winter," I said, listening to the sweet song.

We passed under the arbor of roses and entered a rose garden. At the center of the space was a tall fountain. Around it sat four benches, and on every side, roses blossomed in a variety of hues. Blossoms in yellow, pale pink, fiery red, and even a soft white with a pale pink hue, grew all around.

"Amazing how one can fool Mother Nature," I said, stopping to smell one of the yellow roses.

John leaned in beside me to smell one of the blossoms. When he pulled back, he set a quick kiss on my cheek.

Taking my hand, he led me to a bench. With his free hand, he unbuttoned his coat. "What do you think?" he asked, stroking his finger across my knuckles.

"I love it," I said wistfully. If this place truly belonged to the crown, then I was enjoying the garden of a king. Such a thing was...unthinkable.

"Are you fond of flowers?"

I smiled. "Aren't all women?"

He laughed. "You're right. I just...I hoped you would enjoy this place."

Oh no. I bit my lip. Stupid, Elyse. "John, it's remarkable. I only meant to say that all women—"

He chuckled then set his finger on my lips, silencing me. "My dear, no apology is needed. I understood your jest. I just hope you are happy. I'm quite fond of gardens, of flowers. I hate winter."

I smiled. "My grandmother grew a beautiful flower box outside the window of our flat. She and Missus Murray, Doctor Murray's grandmother, worked the whole spring and summer to grow the most beautiful flowers. My grandmother nursed roses around the window of my garret. I remember their fragrance, and their thorns, very well."

"Your grandmother. The ballerina?"

I nodded.

"Your parents?"

"They...they died when I was very young. I was raised by my grandmother."

"How long have you been on your own?"

"Three years. My grandmother passed away, and then Doctor Murray's grandmother passed a month after. Doctor Murray and I helped one another after that."

"But you and Doctor Murray are not related."

I chuckled. "Oh, no. We are friends. More like family. We support one another."

John nodded, a slight squint creeping across his face. Was he worried I had a romantic attachment to Kai? Perhaps he thought our friendship was beyond propriety? I chewed my lip again. What would someone like him think of a low-born girl like me and her friendship and, really, dependency on a man to whom she was not related?

"It is good of Doctor Murray to watch over you. As young and as beautiful as you are and without family..." he said, his words faltering at the end as if he wanted to say more but did not. "Shall we go around more? I understand there is some exquisite statuary."

I nodded.

Linking his arm in mine, we toured the place, pausing, it seemed, to smell every flower. It was such a heavenly escape, and the time passed very quickly.

John took out his pocket watch. "I'm sorry. We have to go now."

We walked back to the door of the herbarium, stopping to button up once more.

"The warmth was wonderful, but we'll feel ten times colder once we go outside now," John said.

"Well, we'll carry that sunshine in our hearts, like a little ember to keep us warm until spring."

John paused and gently pulled me toward him. "Ember? No. Since the moment I laid eyes on you, a torrent has swept through my heart. The mere thought of you provokes an inferno," he said then leaned toward me.

I returned his kiss, letting the passion I'd been holding inside me loose. I fell into the softness of his mouth, felt the heat emanating from his body, and pulled him close to me. The feel of my breasts pressed against him, the curves of my hips pressed toward him...it was terrible to bear. Longing made me ache.

"But infernos devour you," I said between kisses, my heart beating hard.

He kissed my face, then his lips moved lower, and he drizzled kisses down my neck.

A soft groan escaped my lips. "John...John, I—"

He covered my mouth with his once more. Between kisses, he asked, "Will you meet with me…will you…will you come to me?"

I understood his question. He wanted me, and I could not deny that I wanted him as well. "Yes," I whispered.

"Shall I come to you tonight?" he asked.

"No," I said, suddenly feeling alarmed. The thought of Kai seeing John in my garret apartment filled me with intense shame. All at once, I realized I'd made a mistake. "I…I'm sorry. I spoke hastily. I cannot," I said, feeling embarrassed.

John, who'd gone back to kissing my neck, stopped. He exhaled deeply then set his forehead against my shoulder. "You're right," he said. "I don't know what I was thinking. I…I cannot afford the scandal if we are discovered, and I was wrong to push. You know my intentions toward you are honorable. It…it can wait a bit more."

"Barely," I said with a soft smile, stroking his hair.

"Indeed," he said with a laugh. "Barely."

He took my hand and kissed it. "Best put on your gloves."

I nodded and pulled them from my pocket while John pulled on his hat and gloves. Holding the door open for me, we headed through the second set of doors then outside. There, the old gardener waited. His eyes were focused down the lane.

We turned to see another carriage pulling up behind ours.

I looked at John who squinted at the newcomers, an irritated expression on his face.

"Come on," he said. Taking my hand, he led me toward the carriage.

Behind us, the new arrivals laughed merrily as they got out of their carriage. Out of the corner of my eye, I saw a well-dressed man and woman approach. The man, who had a slight limp, walked with a cane. His voice, a sultry baritone, sounded familiar.

John got into the carriage beside me and took up the reins. Was he trying to leave quickly?

The man and woman stopped beside our carriage.

"Good afternoon," the woman called, giggling merrily.

Frowning, John lowered the reins.

I turned and found myself staring into the face of a tall, slender woman in an expensive-looking coat. Straw-colored curls stuck out from under her bonnet. She smiled at me, a wide toothy grin. Her round stomach gave away that she was with child. Beside her stood Lord Byron.

"Good afternoon," I said politely, quickly turning my attention away from the poet. I hoped he would not remember me.

"I see we aren't the only ones looking for a little warmth today," Byron said, a smirk in his voice. "Lord Byron, and this is my sister, Augusta Leigh. How do you do?" Byron said, tipping his hat politely.

I turned to John.

"Lord Waldegrave, and this is Miss McKenna," he said as he fussed with the reins.

"Miss McKenna," Byron said, considering. "Ah, Miss Elyse McKenna. Of course. How could I forget such a beauty? I simply struggled to place you. You are an actress at the Struthers Theatre, no?"

"Yes, My Lord."

"Isn't she lovely?" Byron asked his sister who continued to give me her toothy grin. "I saw her enact Ophelia. Not just a beauty, but she is also an artist. I had tears in my eyes when you drowned, Miss McKenna," he said with a smile. Lord Byron seemed to have forgotten that he'd also met me on the street after that show and tried to persuade me to come with him for a drink.

"I thank you for your mourning," I said with a wry grin.

Byron smiled at that. "Oh, indeed. Your beauty has given me much to mourn," he said then winked at me. No. He had not forgotten. "And did you say...Lord Waldegrave?" Byron asked, looking past me to John.

John nodded. "Indeed."

Byron seemed to study his face closely. He lifted one eyebrow then smirked. "Indeed."

"I'm afraid Miss McKenna has a performance so we must be on our way. Do enjoy the roses," John said, gripping the reins once more. "Lord Byron. Miss Leigh."

Byron nodded to me then turned with his sister to speak to the gardener.

We rode away from the herbarium down the long, snowy drive. The sun shone softly, casting a glimmer on the snow and ice making it shine with incandescent hues.

"Isn't it beautiful?" I said, motioning to the snow.

John nodded, but he had a distracted look on his face.

Did Byron know his family? Was he worried that Byron would talk behind him? Surely not. The infamous Lord Byron, whom Lady Caroline Lamb had called mad, bad, and dangerous to know, was hardly one to spread rumors when his own behavior was so ill-reputed.

"John?" I said, setting my hand on his knee. "Is anything the matter?"

"Not at all," he said, exhaling deeply. "Lord Bryon is just…well, it's no matter."

I laughed. "Oh my dear, don't worry. Lord Byron is such a rogue. Did you know he asked me to join him for a drink once? As if I were that type of lady. Don't worry about him. I am very certain he won't gossip about you. Men like that know how to keep quiet," I said, guessing at his concern.

"I'm counting on it," John replied, then snapped the reins once more.

12
THE CHEESE

IT WAS LATE AFTERNOON WHEN we returned to the Ice House Theatre. The crowd at the Frost Fair seemed even larger. That night, we were going to have a packed show. I just hoped the Thames could hold everyone in one place. I suddenly envisioned the river giving way underneath us and the lot of us going down. It was an image that made me laugh and sent a shiver down my spine.

"Will you be by for the performance tonight?" I asked John as he lowered me from the carriage.

"I'm afraid I have to go into the city to check on my father. I may not be able to make it, but I'll see you as soon as I can," he said earnestly, brushing a stray strand of my hair behind my ear.

"Promise?"

"Promise," he replied, squeezing my hand.

I looked deeply into his eyes. "Thank you for today, for sharing summer in winter with me."

"Did you really like it?" he asked, a tremor of excitement—or nervousness—in his voice.

I nodded.

He smiled happily. "Then we'll have to go again. But for now..." he said, looking back toward the carriage.

"I'll see you soon," I said then stepped back.

John got back into the carriage, and with a wave, he drove off.

I HEADED BACK TO THE tent to get ready. My stomach growled hungrily, reminding me that I had not yet had dinner.

I stopped by Lizzie's changing area before I went to my section. "Lizzie, has Doctor Murray been by?" I asked.

She cocked her head in thought. "No. I haven't seen him."

I frowned. Certainly, he wasn't still with the pretty captain, was he? The thought annoyed me. No, surely he wasn't. Maybe he'd gone by to the Hawkings' workshop to see the man who'd fallen into the river.

I was turning to leave when Amy and Hannah ran into the tent, both of them breathless.

"Elyse! Lizzie! Look, look," Amy gushed, pushing a piece of paper at me.

Lizzie stood up.

Scanning the pamphlet, I read aloud.

"By the proclamation of Lord Winter

And the authority of Jack Frost

We do hereby declare

The Frost Fair shall crown a winter queen

The most noted lady on the ice

Fairest of this frozen land

Shall be crowned Frostiana

At noon tomorrow

She shall take her throne in the castle of ice

And lord over our kegs, cakes, and meats

All eligible snow maidens should attend

The Frost Fair Prince will choose his Queen

She shall win our admiration and good will

And a trove of the treasures from our frozen land."

"How delightful," Amy shrieked happily. "We should all go. Surely, we are the most well-known maidens on the Thames."

"Us and the tarts at The Frozen Mushroom," Hannah said with a wicked grin, referring to the brothel that had opened on the ice.

"What are you on about now?" Marion asked, joining us.

I looked up at her. It was very obvious she had heard us and her interest was piqued, but she was too sour to say so.

I handed the pamphlet to her.

After reading it over, she puffed her breath through her lips. "Silliness."

"Except that part about a trove of treasures," Lizzie said. "What do you think the prize might be?"

I shook my head.

"Wait, who is the Frost Fair Prince?" Hannah asked.

"Probably some fat lub who concocted this thing just to get silly girls to kiss him," Marion said. She pushed the pamphlet to Lizzie then went back to her wardrobe.

Amy rolled her eyes. "Shall we go?" she asked Lizzie, Hannah, and me.

"I...I will go to Saddlers in the morning, but I should be back by then," Lizzie said, apprehension in her voice. I could tell she was trying not to hurt us by reminding us of her good fortune.

"Perfect," I said with a smile. "With Lizzie's luck this week, perhaps she can win us a case of frozen tripe."

Lizzie smiled at me.

Amy laughed. "We'll have a fish fry to celebrate our Frost Queen."

"And all the land rejoiced when chips were added," I said.

Everyone giggled.

"Ladies, thirty minutes until curtain," Marve called from the front of the tent.

I gave Lizzie's arm a squeeze and with a smile, headed back to my section. I sat down in front of the mirror and looked at my reflection. Again, my hair had been pulled into a mess from the wind.

"Oh, Elyse. Did you dance with the mice all night?" I could hear my Granny say. It was the stock line she uttered every time she sat down to comb my wild tresses in the morning.

Sadness swept over me. It was a fond memory and a bittersweet one all the same. With Granny gone, I had no other living relative. Well, except for Kai. But Kai was not, in truth, really my relation. One day I would have a family again, my own family.

As my hair fell around my shoulders, I thought about John. The hunger between us had almost caused us to do something terribly rash. One lesson Granny had told me that wasn't so sweet was that gentlemen might dream of bedding an actress, but none would wed her thereafter. I was right to deny John, but how did he feel about it? I hoped it had earned me respect and had not frustrated him too much.

I picked up my brush and ran it through my hair. It was odd how John felt both so close to me and also very distant. The secrecy around our relationship created both allure and tension. I hated to think it, but I would be glad when John's father had passed. If his mother held no reservations, as he said she did not, then there would be no barrier to marriage.

Once more, I set about fixing my hair in the fashion of a winter Titania. Feathers, jewels, and silver flowers adorned my locks. Shivering with cold, I slipped out of my dress and into the blue, silver, and white frock of Titania. Up close, I could see the rips in the cheaply made cloth. The audience, however, could detect none of these imperfections in the faerie queen's wardrobe. I slid on the gossamer wings Marve had fashioned, lovely things made of thin paper. They shimmered beautifully under the lights at Struthers Theatre.

"Hermia," Marve called to the back. "Hippolyta."

I sat down once more to apply my makeup. Marion's voice rose from the front of the tent. I could hear the conversation.

"I want to change Persephone's wardrobe for tomorrow morning," I heard Marion tell Marve. "The dress is too limiting during the dances. It caused…complications."

Marve coughed. I could hear the discomfort in his voice. "No need. Elyse will have the role again tomorrow. You can go back to the faerie godmother."

There was silence for a moment then Marion said. "And that is your final decision?"

"Yes."

There was no further reply. Marion, who knew very well she had mangled the part, would not argue. Her pride would not let her hear the words spoken aloud.

"Hermia?" Marve called to Lizzie.

"Coming," she called.

I finished up my makeup then opened my trunk to take out Titania's silver slippers. I smiled at my pale pink ballet shoes sitting inside. I missed Granny terribly. What would she think of John and the situation I found myself in? What would she advise? It was then I realized that maybe it was fortunate I had not talked to Kai about my worries that morning. If he'd thought John was off gaming and drinking when he told me he'd be elsewhere, Kai would have tracked him down to demand answers. That would not have gone well at all.

I slipped on Titania's slippers then headed backstage just as the flutes announced the opening of act one.

"Ah, here you are," Marve said. "The crowd is very big tonight. There are many notables out there. Just do your very best, Elyse. Surely someone will notice you and refer you," he said then paused, smiling at me in a fatherly way. "I remember when your grandmother first brought you around for an introduction. I think I'd miss you too much, Elyse. I have half a mind not to let you go on," he said with a soft laugh.

I smiled. "How could I ever leave you? Why don't you amend Puck's epilogue and invite them to visit us at Struthers after the thaw?"

Marve raised his eyebrows and nodded excitedly. "Excellent idea," he said then hurried off to find Anderson.

I tiptoed to my spot just off stage. Hermia was in the midst of an impassioned plea to King Theseus that she be able to wed Lysander. Hippolyta glared at her betrothed from stage right. Well, at least Marion played the defeated Amazon queen very well.

I peered out through the slat in the wood then suppressed a gasp. The crowd extended to the very edges of the audience boundary, and others watched through the open entrance. Seated at the front, the gentry glimmered in their fine gowns and suits. They were out en masse. I scanned the rows for John but didn't see him.

My eyes then flicked to the pole by which Kai had been standing sentinel.

He wasn't there either. I searched the crowd for his familiar brooding face but didn't see him anywhere.

Sighing, I looked away and closed my eyes. No more Elyse. Now I was Titania. I was Titania. My husband and I were in the midst of a quarrel. I had come to see King Theseus wed and only encountered Oberon here by chance. I let myself slip into the role of Titania, so lost in my thoughts that when I took the stage, Elyse had disappeared.

Out of sight, Skippy and Marve worked their wonders, creating a crack of lightning and the roll of thunder as I entered stage left.

As if working in tandem, a sharp wind blew across the frozen Thames. The gust carried crystals of ice. Under the moonlight, they shimmered like prisms of colorful light. From my position on the stage, I saw the wind whip across the crowd. The audience murmured quietly as they held onto their caps. The timing of the effect was perfect.

Oberon, already on stage, scowled angrily at me.

"Ill met by moonlight, proud Titania," Robert growled.

"What, jealous Oberon?" I seethed at him, turning to the audience so they could see my frustrated expression. When I did so, I noticed the foreign gentleman standing just behind the gentry at the center of the audience in his regular spot, his hands resting on his walking stick. Surely he had not been there earlier. Such a striking figure, I was amazed to think I could have missed him.

He nodded to me, just the slightest of movements.

I pulled my attention away before Elyse's interests came too much to the surface. I was not Elyse, I was Titania.

I turned back to the faeries who carried the long train of my dress. "Faeries, skip away. I have forsworn his love and company."

Oberon laughed ruefully. "Rash woman. Aren't I your lord?"

"Then I must be your lady," I said with a sardonic smirk.

And then, I was lost to the faerie queen's devices.

I kept my focus on my lines, my moves, and my mood. I was Titania. My only concerns were that of Titania's. More than once I had to redirect myself as I sought Kai in the crowd, but he was not there. And more than once, I had to force away a blush of pride when the foreign gentleman smiled, laughed, or looked moved by the way I'd tossed a line.

Out of breath, when my final act came once more, I could scarcely believe it. Again, the three pairs of lovers lay on stage. I prepared my pouch of faerie dust and waited for Oberon to signal my cue.

"Sing and dance," Oberon called to the faeries assembled.

I pirouetted onto the stage then stopped and turned to my faeries.

"Hand in hand, faeries, let us spread our grace

We shall sing and bless this place."

With that, I moved again through the sleeping pairs, twirling on the tips of my toes until it hurt, casting Titania's blessings on all the lovers.

When I was done, the faerie train retreated once more, leaving wily Puck on stage to deliver the final speech.

We waited backstage and listened.

I mouthed the words along with Puck. His lines were my favorite in the entire play. I smiled, listening as Puck's final lines came to a close and he called the fine crowd to meet us again:

"Give me your hands, if we be friends,

And Robin shall make amends

And if you delight in our players

Meet us in London at the theatre Struthers"

At that, the crowd broke into applause. We waited for several moments, reveling in the hearty applause, before we all went back on stage to accept our reward. Hand in hand with Robert, I approached the front of the stage and curtseyed. No Kai. No John. The foreign gentleman, however, removed his top hat and bowed to me.

I smiled at him.

After that, we headed to the tent backstage.

"Elyse," Lizzie said, rushing up toward me. "Who is that handsome man with the pale blond hair? Is that the one you mentioned earlier?"

"The rich one," Amy added, joining her.

"His eyes never left you," Lizzie added.

I nodded to Lizzie. "I don't know. I spoke with him but didn't catch his name. He's not an Englishman."

"A foreign lord," Amy said, her eyes looking soft and dreamy. "Maybe his ship is trapped in the Thames."

"I thought the same," I told her.

"But you didn't get his name?" Lizzie asked.

I smiled. "Tomorrow. Tomorrow, I will ask."

"Oh, Elyse. You have all the luck with the gentlemen," Amy said with a sigh.

"It only takes one," I said, setting my hand on her shoulder. "The right one."

Marve arrived backstage. He looked pale. "I'm going to close down the Ice House. I don't care how much I'm making," he said, shaking his head.

"What is it?" Amy and Lizzie asked at once.

Marve looked down at his hand. Therein, he had two slips of paper.

"Robert?" he called.

Robert, who must have already been on his way to see what the matter was, came from the right of the tent where his changing area was located. "Drury Lane," he said, handing a note to the actor.

I looked at the paper in Marve's hands. My stomach shook with excitement. Surely there was a note for me.

"Amy," he said, passing her the other note. "Covent Garden."

Amy gasped then took the paper.

"And for Miss Hannah," Marve said, passing her a bouquet of Frost Fair roses. "There is a gentleman outside who'd like to make your acquaintance."

I smiled at my friends. A terrible sense of jealousy swept over me, but I pushed it down.

"Congratulations," I told Amy and Robert.

"Elyse, tomorrow, surely, someone will—" Lizzie began, but I raised a hand to stop her.

"Someone has to look after Marve," I said. "I can't leave him all alone with Marion."

"Speaking of, where is she?" Robert asked.

"She stormed off right after the play finished," Hannah said.

"I let her know she would not play Persephone tomorrow," Marve explained. "She was angry."

"Forget her. How exciting for you both," I said. "But now, I need to get dressed and find Doctor Murray. He'll want to check on his patient who fell through the ice."

The others nodded then let me go, knowing I was more upset than I let show. I headed back to my area then began pulling off my wardrobe. What did it matter? If I was to wed John, I would likely leave the theatre anyway. It didn't really matter. Maybe I wasn't as talented an actress as I thought I was. I slipped off Titania's gown and opened the trunk to lay it inside when something odd caught my eye.

My pink satin slippers were inside the trunk, but they looked... wrong. I lifted one of the ballet slippers to inspect it. The stitches at the side had frayed apart. When had it worn so thin? But then I looked more closely. No. It was not frayed. Someone had cut a massive hole in the side. I looked at the other slipper. The pink satin ankle sash had been ripped off.

No. Oh no.

I hugged the slippers to my chest.

No.

Marion.

It had to have been Marion.

How could she be so jealous about something so small? To ruin something so precious to me was just...unthinkable.

I tossed the rest of my wardrobe into the chest and locked it. Slipping on my regular clothes and a coat, and pulling on a pair of boots, I got ready to go. I slid my slippers into my bag. They could be repaired, but the toe would never hold steady now. How could she?

I blinked back my tears. On the other side of the tent, Lizzie and Amy were gushing excitedly. I steeled my heart, forcing myself not to envy them, then headed outside. There, I spotted Hannah on the arm of a handsome looking gentleman. From his dress, he looked to be a tradesman of some sort, a man of means but also the kind of man who could marry an actress without any shame, and walk about with her in public without fear of being spotted.

My stomach churned. I headed toward the front of the theatre to look for Kai. There was no one there. I gripped my bag then walked down Freezeland Lane toward The Frozen Mermaid.

The crowd on the Thames was merry. Everyone seemed joyful. Laughing couples, families, groups of young people together, everyone was having fun.

And what about me? Who did I have?

A lover who was ashamed of me.

A friend who was missing.

And no family.

I was an orphan and a Cheapside actress with no talent and no future.

I stopped at the entrance to The Frozen Mermaid and looked inside.

"Miss McKenna?" one of the serving girls said, seeing me linger at the entry.

"Is Doctor Murray here?"

The girl shook her head. "I haven't seen him today."

I nodded politely. "Thank you," I said, and with a frown, I turned and headed in the direction of Captain Behra's ship.

13
ILL MET BY MOONLIGHT

THE SCENE OUTSIDE THE SHIP would have rivaled a festival to Bacchus. All around, the sailors danced with pretty girls while others played the strange assortment of instruments. The music was unlike any I had ever heard before. Torches lit the area surrounding the ship, and wine was being passed around in plenty.

I balked as I neared the scene. It was a rowdy sight. The dancing couples were certainly not keeping within the bounds of propriety. The sailors' hands roved across their partners' breasts and backsides. In the shadow of night amongst the casks, I saw two lovers in the throes of passion. Their soft moans carried on the wind.

"Miss McKenna," a soft voice called.

The young boy, Robin, bounded off the ship toward me. He'd been playing a pan-flute. He was still holding it when he rushed over to me. The glimmer of excitement shone in his eyes.

"Robin," I said with a smile. "I am sorry to bother your...crew."

"Troupe."

"Sorry?"

"We're a troupe. What did you need, Miss McKenna?"

"I was planning to head back into the city, but I'm trying to find Doctor Murray. Do you happen to know where he went when he left Captain Behra?"

"Left? Why, he never left. He's still inside. Shall we check on him?"

"He...he never left?"

Robin smiled mischievously then took my hand. "Come on," he said, leading me back up the plank.

The others gathered there smiled happily at me but kept to their merrymaking. Robin led me on deck to the captain's quarters.

"Captain?" he called, opening the door ajar just slightly. "Miss McKenna wants to see Doctor Murray."

From inside, I heard what sounded like a muffled laugh.

"Send Miss McKenna in," I heard the captain call.

Inside the captain's quarters, the lamps had been dimmed. It was very warm.

"What can I do for you, Miss McKenna?" the captain asked.

It took a moment for my eyes to adjust to the light. When I finally got a fix on her, I saw that she was lying on her cot. I was shocked to see that she was topless. She smiled at me then reached out for a fur coat lying on the floor.

I averted my eyes as she rose, seeing from the periphery that she had, in fact, been entirely naked. She wrapped the coat around her then went to her desk.

"I...I was looking for—"

"Wine?" she asked. She poured a goblet then handed it to me. She had the oddest expression on her face. Though she was smiling, there was so much anger buried behind that smile that I couldn't quite understand how the two emotions could be contained on one visage.

"I...no...is...was Doctor—"

"Kai?" the captain said, turning back toward her cot.

I turned then to see Kai lying there nestled under the blankets. His coat was off, the front of his shirt undone. He was fast asleep.

"Kai?" I whispered.

"He's not used to our wine," the captain said, setting down the goblet she'd offered to me. "He'll need some sleep, I think. He's quite worn thin."

I could feel the flush on my cheeks, anger and embarrassment mixing together.

"Kai," I demanded. "Have you lost your mind?" Fury swept over me. What was he...what had he done?

"Elyse?" he called sleepily, but he didn't rise. He sounded confused.

"Best let him sleep it off," the captain said. "Unless you might like to stay as well," she said, letting her coat slip casually from her shoulder, giving the briefest glimpse of her breast. "I suspect he might enjoy that."

I gasped. Furious, I turned and stormed out of the captain's cabin. Outside, the revelry continued, but Robin was nowhere to be seen.

Behind me, the captain laughed.

My cheeks burned. I headed down the plank and back onto the ice. As I walked back into the darkness, hot tears trailed down my cheeks.

Kai had a right to his own life. He could do whatever he wanted, but still. It was…I was…I felt sick. I moved quickly through the crowd, tears wetting my cheeks. My emotions tumbled over themselves. How could Kai just bed that woman like that? Apparently, I didn't know him at all. I'd always thought he was too fine a man for something like that. And for that woman to ask me to join them…well, I could barely believe what I had heard. Fury and sorrow racked me. I gripped my bag, the ruined slippers inside, then headed back toward town. At the very least, I could make some use of myself and attend to his patient. Clearly Kai had been unable to do so. At that moment, I was so very sorry that I didn't know how to reach John. I needed him. I needed someone.

My eyes wet with tears, I walked blindly. My mind was reeling so feverishly that I was lost to myself. I came to a sharp halt, however, when I walked right into someone.

I staggered backward, more mortified than ever.

"Oh my goodness. I'm so sorry. I was—" I began, but then stopped when I realized who I'd crashed into. The foreign gentleman was there, steadying me by the arms so I wouldn't fall.

"Miss McKenna," he said, looking surprised. He looked closely at my face, seeming to take in my distress. "What's happened?"

"I..." I began, looking back in the direction of the ship. "Nothing," I said, dashing the tears from my cheeks.

The foreign gentleman followed my gaze. He frowned hard. "Are you hurt?"

"Oh, no," I said with a gasp. "Just a bit upset. My friend..." I said, looking back once more. "It's nothing."

"You've had an argument with your friend?"

"Just...a misunderstanding. It's nothing. I'm terribly sorry."

The foreign gentleman glared at the ship once more then offered me his arm. "Miss McKenna, I believe I failed to make an introduction. I'm Baron Moren," he said. "And it would be my pleasure to escort you home."

I took a deep, shuddering breath. A baron? The girls were right, I was swimming in gentlemen...all the wrong gentlemen.

"Thank you. I...I was planning to visit some friends who live along the Thames. It's not a far walk. Would you mind?"

"Not at all. I'm sorry to see you in such a state, Miss McKenna. Especially after your fine performance tonight."

I took the baron's arm. "I'm glad you enjoyed it," I said, trying to calm myself. The last thing I needed to do was make any more of a fool of myself.

"You play Titania very well. Her words evoke sympathy when coming from your lips. A trick unfamiliar to most Titanias. You play her earnestly."

"I try to imagine her sorrow at the quarrel between her and her king."

"Does she feel sorrow? I always thought her argument to be petty."

"Oh, no," I said. "At the end of the play, she professes her deep love for Oberon. I think she appears so angry because she loves him so deeply and their quarrel wounds her. In my mind, she wants nothing more than to be with him but is too prideful to find a way."

"I never considered it from that point of view."

"Of course, Oberon is no better. He loves her as well. His spite hurts them both."

The baron nodded thoughtfully but said nothing.

"Do they enact much of the Bard's work where you live?" I asked, hoping my ignorance of his barony wasn't completely obvious. I still had no idea where, exactly, the gentleman was from.

"No," he said with a smile. "But we are quite familiar with Titania."

I nodded, unsure what to make of his comment.

"Perhaps we shall see you as Persephone tomorrow?"

"Yes. In the morning," I said, gripping my bag once more. "Assuming the river is still frozen," I added, trying to soften the mood.

He smiled. "She'll hold at least another two days, I believe."

"And will you return home then or do you have more business in London?"

"We shall see."

It was clear then that I'd found the limit of that conversation.

We turned off the ice and walked down the cobblestone road toward the Hawkings' workshop. I cast a look out at the Frost Fair. The whole river was alive with excitement. Laughter, music, and lights danced across the frozen Thames.

"It is a lovely scene," I said, casting my hand toward the river.

"The Thames is beautiful in all her seasons. But this is a sight to behold. It's been nineteen years since the last Frost Fair. It's amazing how much merrymaking a bit of ice can provide. Though I think your company is the first ever to perform on the river. It's splendid."

I smiled at him. "We play at the Struthers Theatre year round. You'll have to visit us there after the ice melts."

At that, he smiled but said nothing.

Shortly thereafter, we arrived at the Hawkings' workshop. The entire house was lit up, and from inside, I heard the sounds of clanging metal and an odd popping sound.

"My friends are tinkers. Quite skilled, really, if a bit eccentric."

"All the best people are," he said then let me go.

He waited while I inquired at the door. A moment later, the Hawkings' footman waved me inside.

"Thank you so much for escorting me," I told the baron. I didn't know how to express to him how much his kindness meant to me after such an upsetting night.

He removed his hat and bowed to me, his long blond hair falling forward when he did so. "It was my pleasure," he said. "I hope to see you again, Miss McKenna. And, next time, with a smile rather than tears."

He had seen my distress, and he had cared. It moved me greatly. "Thank you."

With a nod, he turned and headed back into the night.

14
MANNERLY GENTLEMAN

"MISS MCKENNA," ISABELLE CALLED HAPPILY from the top of the staircase. She waved then came thundering down the steps. I had to look twice when I realized that under her apron she was, in fact, wearing trousers. As she descended, she craned her neck to look around me. Not seeing Kai there, she frowned but then quickly smothered her disappointment.

"How good of you to come," she said, panting when she got to the bottom of the stairs. "Father is working in the basement. Is...will Doctor Murray be joining you? We haven't seen him today."

"One of the ship captains was injured. He's needed on the ice," I said, masking my worry. It was not quite the truth but good enough. "I came in his stead. I thought I could call on the gentleman."

"Oh, you should. He's making a marvelous recovery. The Bow Street Runners were here today. They think we may have a lead on identifying him. Someone is coming in the morning to pay him a visit."

"Really?"

Isabelle nodded. "A gentleman went missing some days back. His family has been searching for him. We'll see in the morning. Now come, you'll want to say hello to my father," she said, pulling me by the arm. She headed toward a door leading to the basement, pausing to scoop up a pile of books sitting on the floor by the door. "Watch your step, and don't mind the smell."

"Smell?"

Without another word, Isabelle led us downstairs. "Papa?" she called. "Papa, we have a visitor."

"Ah, Doctor Murray at last," Master Hawking replied followed by the sound of metal clattering. There was a strange odor coming from the basement, an odd mix of sulfur and vinegar.

"Oh, no. He's not here. Miss McKenna has come."

"She's not...you didn't bring here down here, did you?" I heard him ask a second before I turned the corner.

I understood his hesitation the moment I did so. On two long slabs, Master Hawking had cadavers laid out. Their delicate parts were covered, but the pale corpses lay exposed to the open air. That, at least, explained the smell.

"Isabelle," Master Hawking said, chiding his daughter softly. "You must remember that not all ladies—" he began then sighed. "Some ladies have softer sensibilities, my dear. Miss McKenna," he said, bowing to me.

"I may be an artist, sir, but I assure you that the human body does not frighten me. I'm afraid I've spent too many years at Doctor Murray's side. I've quite gotten over any nerves." Despite my bravado, I swallowed hard.

Master Hawking smiled then turned to the tables and his nearby workbench. "Doctor Murray and I have been working many months on ways to help the wounded," he said then waved me to his workbench.

Isabelle hopped up on a nearby table to watch. "Do you remember the optics I showed you upstairs?" she asked.

I nodded.

Master Hawking tapped a glass jar filled with eyeballs then reached out and picked up one of the optics Isabelle had shown me. "Better than a glass eye, but not yet as effective as I had hoped," he said then set it down. "This, however," he said, picking up an odd-looking ball inside a joint, "has shown promise."

"What is it?" I asked.

"A knee," he replied. "Well, at least the knee joint. Two canine trials have already proven successful."

I stared from the machine to the man. "How?"

He laughed heartily and set the tinkered contraption back down. "Imagine it like this. Once the new, metal bones are set, the body will grow vines around it, holding it in place. That is the beauty. We also use nuts, bolts, screws, and clamping." He then lifted an odd-looking bagpipe. "And this. Can you guess?"

I shook my head.

He inhaled deeply, let out a big breath, then breathed in again. After he exhaled he said, "No more death by consumption. I can repair or replace the lungs."

"But Master Hawking…that's impossible."

"Oh no, my dear. I assure you, it's quite possible. Doctor Murray understands the body. I understand the machine. When the two meet…"

"It's a perfect match," Isabelle said, and this time I heard a wistfulness in her voice that made something mean in me tighten. Perhaps she wouldn't think Kai was so perfect if she knew he was passed out drunk, and half naked, in the ship of a foreign captain.

"It is truly a marvel," I said then turned and looked at the bodies. The two men, both young, gone before their years, were pale as milk, their skin blue all around the edges.

"Ah, my subjects," Master Hawking said. "I'd appreciate your discretion on that matter, Miss McKenna. I'm sure you know acquiring subjects for research is a delicate matter."

By delicate, of course, he meant illegal. I had to wonder what role Kai might have taken in procuring the bodies.

"Of course," I said with a smile.

"Will we be expecting Doctor Murray tonight?" Master Hawking asked.

"He's busy on the ice," Isabelle explained then jumped back down.

I nodded. "I wanted to come check on his patient."

"Fine man. He's recovering very well," Master Hawking said then turned to Isabelle. "Be sure to have some tea made for Miss McKenna. You must be frozen to the bone."

"Thank you. That's very kind."

Isabelle waved for me to follow her. "Come on," she said with a smile.

"Thank you for showing me your work, Master Hawking. It's quite amazing."

The old man smiled a wide and toothy grin. He nodded to me.

Following Isabelle back upstairs, I pressed my gloved hand to my nose and tried to root out the smell, replacing it with the soft perfume that scented my clothes.

"Why don't you go up?" Isabelle said, pointing to the stairs. "I'll come in a few minutes with some tea."

I smiled. The Hawkings were very charming, but their manners were so out of the ordinary that I hardly knew what to do.

Without waiting for me to reply, Isabelle turned toward the kitchen.

I went upstairs and down the hallway to the room where the gentleman was resting. I paused when I got to the door. It was highly irregular for a lady to enter a gentleman's chamber unchaperoned. I knocked softly on the door.

"Sir?" I called.

"Yes?"

"Sir, it's Miss McKenna. If you are up for a visit, I thought to check on you. I'm very sorry, but I have no chaperone. I wasn't sure…"

On the other side of the door, the gentleman laughed. "Come in, Miss McKenna."

I opened the door carefully and went inside. The room was well-lit. The gentleman sat in his bed, a book lying open on his lap. His color was much improved, a blush of pink in his cheeks.

"Sir," I said, curtseying when I entered.

He smiled and waved for me to draw close. "Kind people, the Hawkings. Not the most formal, I must admit."

"No, sir," I said with a smile then pulled a chair alongside his bed. "You're looking much better."

"I'm feeling much better. The feeling in my legs has returned. I even had a turn about the room today. The local surgeon Doctor Murray has checking on me is very knowledgeable. I had hoped to see Doctor Murray today. Is he here?"

"I'm sorry, he is attending to an injured patient on the Thames," I lied again. Once more, my stomach clenched hard. I swallowed my upset and smiled serenely.

The man nodded. "And you, Miss McKenna, how was your day? What did you enact?"

"This evening, I played the role of Titania. This morning, however, I took on the role of the faerie godmother in *Glass Slipper Girl*."

"Ah, yes. I remember that tale well. My governess used to read it to me."

"You had a governess?" I asked.

He raised an eyebrow. "Apparently so," he said in surprise which made us both laugh. "But Miss McKenna, why do I remember you as a ballerina? Do you dance?"

"I do indeed," I replied. I opened my bag and pulled out one of my soft pink ballet slippers. "I was trained in ballet by my grandmother."

"May I?" he asked, reaching out for the slipper.

I handed it to him. As he looked it over, he smiled. "The material is silk. It is old, but a fine quality. The dye is well done. The stitches...did someone do this to your slipper intentionally?"

"Isn't it interesting that you know so much on the fabrics?" I said, avoiding the question. I felt embarrassed and annoyed that I was embarrassed. It wasn't my fault Marion was an evil shrew.

The gentleman raised an inquisitive eyebrow at me but said nothing. "I've spent all day noticing each piece of linen in this room, examining its weave and color. Much to my surprise, I can tell you everything about these fabrics and where many of the bolts came from."

"Then we must put out a call amongst the haberdashers and hosiers."

"Master Hawking was kind enough to send out inquiries earlier today. I don't mean to press, but I notice that you did not answer my other inquiry,

Miss McKenna," he said, looking at the rip on the side of my slipper.

"You're right. My apologies. I felt a bit embarrassed. Alas, that is the handiwork of a rival actress," I explained.

He signed heavily. "I am sorry to hear such an injustice was done to you."

"Thank you, sir. It's no matter. They are very old and worn and needed to be replaced anyway."

"Indeed, which makes me suspect you kept them for a reason."

"Whomever you are, sir, you are quite perceptive," I said with a smile which made him laugh.

"Only concerned. I owe you and Doctor Murray my life, Miss McKenna. It pains me to think anyone would harm you. Once I remember who I am, I am very certain I shall have quite the debt to repay."

"Think nothing of it," I said, setting my hand gently on his arm. I was surprised to find the muscles underneath were very firm.

He took my hand and squeezed it very gently, his blue eyes soft as he smiled at me.

"Tea?" Isabelle called from the doorway as she entered with a tray.

I pulled my hand back.

"Is she wearing trousers?" the gentleman asked under his breath.

I chuckled.

"No, thank you, Miss Hawking. I'll never sleep if I take tea so late," he told her.

"Miss McKenna."

"Please. After spending all day on the ice, I still feel chilled."

Isabelle poured a cup, ladened it with sugar, then handed it to me. Taking a cup for herself, she sat on the end of the bed and took a sip. "Is that your ballet slipper?" she asked, looking at the gentleman's hands.

I nodded.

Setting her cup down, she rose. She took my cup from my hand and set it aside.

"You must teach me a step or two," she said, pulling me to an open space.

"Now?"

"Why not?"

The gentleman chuckled.

"Very well," I said. "Let's begin. Take your first position like this," I said, modeling the arrangement of my feet.

Isabelle copied my movements.

"Now, let me show you a simple plié," I said, showing her the move which she imitated in a graceful manner. Despite her unkempt attire, she really was a lovely girl. Her curling dark hair was accentuated by her wide, dark eyes.

"How is that?" she asked.

The gentleman clapped. "You have it, Miss Hawking."

"If you should ever like a real lesson, we can arrange it. You could come to Struthers Theatre."

She smiled. "What a sweet offer. I am so busy right now helping Papa work on the wedding commissions but maybe afterward."

I nodded then lifted my cup of tea once more, this time polishing it off. My stomach full of the warm liquid, I determined it was time to take my leave.

"I must be heading home before it gets too late," I said.

The gentleman smiled. "It was very kind of you to stop by. Thank you."

"I'll return tomorrow. Can I bring you anything?"

He shook his head. "No. Thank you."

"Some onion soup, perhaps?"

He laughed. "I think I've had a lifetime's worth."

Grinning, I curtseyed to him, and turning to Isabelle, we both headed back downstairs.

"You will tell Doctor Murray we were sorry we didn't see him today?" Isabelle said as she followed me to the door.

"Of course. I'm sure he's sorry he was not able to make a call."

She nodded, her expression hiding her disappointment very poorly. Perhaps she would make a graceful dancer, but her face was far too honest for the theatre.

I fastened my coat once more, and with a wave, I headed back out into the night. The chilly air bit my nose. All at once, I was overcome with tiredness. I wanted nothing more than to be back in my little garret apartment.

Following the twisting cobblestones, I finally found my way home once more. It was so foggy, I hadn't seen a soul on my path there. The loneliness of it filled me with disquiet. Once I was inside my flat, the feeling did not ease. I lit the fire then pulled off my day clothes in favor of a dressing gown. The window of Kai's garret was dark. He wasn't home. Soon, my fire was burning warmly. Wrapping my blanket around my shoulders, I crawled up on the little ledge beside the window and stared at the darkened frame of Kai's window. A sick feeling racked my stomach. I closed my eyes and tried to remember all the good that had happened today, to remember the summer in winter John had shown me, the taste of his kiss, and the sweetness of his words. But no matter how hard I tried to focus on him, my eyes returned again and again to the dark window and the terrible sense of dread that washed over me.

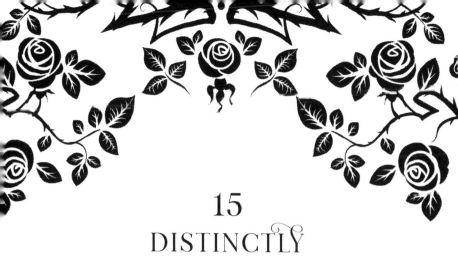

15
DISTINCTLY
FEMININE DRAGONS

I WOKE THE NEXT MORNING feeling tired after a night full of fitful dreams. The sun had just risen over the horizon. My fire had burnt low, and it was terribly cold in the apartment. I pulled my blankets around me. Rubbing my hands together, I knelt by the stove to rekindle the fire. When the work was done, I rose and went to the window. Kai's flat was still dark. I slipped on my boots, not bothering to lace them, then pulled on my coat. I went to the window and undid the latch. Moving carefully, I crawled out onto the roof.

A wind whipped hard across the London rooftops, carrying with it the terrible chill that had frozen the Thames. I went to Kai's window. Grabbing the metal handle, the deep chill of the freezing metal biting my hand, I pushed the window open and looked inside.

"Kai?" I called. The flat, which was no larger than my own, could be taken in in one glance. But still, it unnerved and surprised me to find it empty. I slipped inside.

His little garret apartment was a mirror of my own. The only difference was that his grandmother, who had been talented with art, had painted the walls with flowers, birds, and swirling designs. I glanced around the room to find Kai's small bed was still made.

My hand dancing close to his stove, I felt no heat. I opened the grate and looked inside. There wasn't even an ember still warm within. The fire had grown cold. Kai had not been home since we'd left yesterday morning.

Panic swept over me, and my heart beat hard. It was unlike Kai to be so impulsive. He was a man whose days ran like a clock. As a girl, I had chided him because he would never dare risky adventures. Kai was serious and thoughtful. Maybe I flattered myself to think he wouldn't be so callous as to leave me worrying about him like this. Maybe I didn't fall as high in his esteem as I thought. Was I simply his childhood playmate? A neighbor? A poor orphaned girl for whom he felt sympathy? Maybe now that John had made his intentions clear, Kai didn't feel like he had to worry about me anymore. The captain *was* very attractive, and Kai was unattached. Surely he had a right to his dalliances. What business was it of mine anyway? But if it wasn't my business, why did I feel so miserable?

A tear slipped down my cheek.

The image of Kai lying on the captain's cot, his shirt undone, and the captain naked, rolled through my mind. My stomach clenched. It seemed unthinkable that Kai had been intimate with another woman.

Another woman?

Other than me.

What?

I lay down on his cot. What a ridiculous notion. I didn't own Kai. He was like a brother to me. I just wanted the best for him, that was all. I just wanted him to be happy, but getting drunk and rolling around with a lusty ship captain was just so out of character and entirely unacceptable. Kai was so much better than that. He was smart, handsome, kind, and loving. He was quite perfect, his surly nature aside. But I loved him for that. It was part of what made him who he was. How could he just throw himself away on a wanton woman instead of someone proper, someone who truly cared for him?

Someone like me.

The thought struck me hard.

No. No, it was not like that. I was in love with John. John had set my world afire. His love was like an inferno burning its way through my life. We were just waiting for the moment to be together.

But if my love was so absolute, why did my feelings for Kai seem so confused? Was I just being jealous? That was ridiculous, wasn't it?

I breathed in deeply. I could still smell Kai's cherry-scented soap clinging to his bed linens. The smell, mixed with the heady masculine musk, was divine. It was like being with him.

It occurred to me then that if I married John, I would rarely see Kai. I wouldn't have his company, his garret window across from my own, his smell to comfort me.

I rolled onto my back and looked up at the images painted on the ceiling above Kai's bed. His grandmother had painted a window trimmed all around with vining red roses. And outside his window, she had painted an elaborate dragon perched on top of a castle, a plume of fire rolling from his mouth. Standing before the castle was a boy holding a wooden sword. Gram had painted Kai's nine-year-old likeness.

I smiled at the image. A tear slipped from the corner of my eye into my ear. If I couldn't stand one night without Kai across from my garret window, how could I stand a lifetime?

I rose and wiped away my tear. Maybe Kai was entitled to his own life, but not like this. If Gram were here, she would take Kai by the ear and drag him away from Captain Behra's ship. But since she wasn't here, it was up to me to keep Kai from danger. That woman was like the dragon breathing fire, a dangerous inferno. Kai was too good to see the evil and mischief in others. But to me, her ill-intentions were all too apparent. It was time to put out the flames.

16
WHAT ELYSE HEARD

THE EARLY MORNING SUNRISE LIT the sky with shades of pink and purple. The ice on the Thames glimmered beautifully, reflecting the opalescent rays of the sun. The image of it reminded me of the inside of a clam shell, pearly white with a rainbow of pastel hues. The magnificence of the image, as if the Thames had been dipped into an enchanted glow, could not have been more in contrast with my sour mood. Inside me, I railed back and forth between Kai and the captain, then at myself for my senseless fury, then back again. At times, my anger even levied itself at John, who seemed to have no good reason to treat me like some tart he should keep secret. I might have been a woman with a profession, but that did not make me a harlot. My bitterness spilled over to Marion and her petty jealousies. And once more, my anger would shift again to Kai.

Since it was early in the morning, life on the icy Thames was just beginning to stir. Fires were being rekindled, wagons with fresh loads of ale were rolling in from the city, and the vendors opening their tents for the day yawned open-mouthed as they nursed steaming cups of tea. I frowned at the pleasant images, angry with them for being in such sharp contrast to my anger, then set my sights on the foreign ship. If Kai was still there, I would take him by the scruff and drag him home.

Overnight, several more tents had cropped up on the ice near where the ship was docked. I dodged through a row of tents which lined the space, stepping over piles of timber and rope. I was just about to exit the narrow alleyway between the tents when I heard the sound of voices. A man and woman were having a heated argument.

No, not just any man and woman. It was Captain Behra. But the other voice struck me as familiar as well.

Standing beside one of the tents, I stopped for a moment and listened.

"I'll have no more of this, Tia. Send him away," the gentleman said.

"Or what?" the captain replied with a snort. Tia? Was that her first name?

"Or you know what. Two can play at this game."

"You started this in the first place, mooning over her. Did you want to make me jealous? You didn't even think about me until I took a lover."

"Took a lover?" the man said with a hard laugh. "You have taken a love, which is far crueler."

"What do you know of love?"

"Much. Which is why you need to let him go."

"Then you must agree to cease your affections as well."

"There is no affection, merely admiration. If you were not so proud, you would be able to see that. Are you so low that you cannot admire another woman's gifts?"

"Gifts? Is that what you're calling those pert breasts? Those pale cheeks?"

"I have no interest in her breasts, cheeks, or anything else. Jealous, Tia, you're making excuses so you can delight in mortal flesh. And how have you come by it? Through trickery and drunkenness and for what, a petty slight?"

"Petty? Petty? You call me petty? You are the one who is petty. You are the one who has done wrong."

"Again, I have no affection for any woman save my wife. Admiration, yes? Esteem, yes? But no one owns my love save you."

"Pretty words."

"Truth, my Tia. Let us make amends. Give me what I want and I shall leave this place."

"What you want?"

"My son."

The woman laughed. "You lost him fairly. Is all this...are all these games, these taunts, because of Robin?"

There was no reply.

"How dare you," the woman stammered. "How dare you play with me over such a thing? I will not be ruled by you, not now, and never again. I do not believe your pretty words. I will crush you and your *esteemed* girl. And I will break her love between my thighs until he has forgotten her."

The captain said no more. I caught sight of her as she headed back across the ice toward her ship.

Left behind, the unseen gentleman sighed then turned. From the sound of his footfalls, he was headed my way.

I suppressed a yelp then turned and ducked into one of the tents. My heart thundered in my chest as I gripped the fabric of the tent door. I cast a hasty glance behind me to find two workmen fast asleep inside. The tent stank of ale and body odor.

Taking a deep breath, I peered out the crack of the tent door.

I bit my lip when the baron walked by.

The captain and the baron were lovers? Were married? And for some reason still unclear to me, they were quarreling. The child, Robin, seemed to be the reason. Was he really their son? But more, were they talking about Kai and me? Was I the girl the baron esteemed? Had she trapped Kai because of me? A dragon indeed, and a dangerous one at that.

I needed to get Kai out of there. But I would need help.

Making sure that the baron was far out of sight, I dashed out of the tent. Happy to take in a breath of unspoiled air, I filled my lungs with the frosty morning scent then turned and headed toward the Ice House Theatre. The men in my company were not soldiers, but they were not to be trifled with either. I would have to enlist their help if I had any hope of retrieving Kai. The captain's plan exposed, I knew my old friend needed my help more than ever.

As I headed back toward the Ice House, I replayed the conversation I'd overheard again and again in my mind. The captain had been so cruel to the baron who had been nothing but kind and gentle. Why did some women become so rough? What happened to make them lose their softness? Was there any way to mend their frozen hearts? Perhaps the answer to retrieving Kai was not in a show of force. I stopped then turned around, heading back in the direction toward which I'd seen the baron travel. Even the Thames would eventually melt under the warmth of the sun. Maybe the captain could as well. The gentleman had been nothing but kind to me. Was there a way I could help him make amends?

I rushed down the ice. I turned a corner and spotted the baron. He marched angrily toward the other end of the river, away from the captain. Lifting my skirts, I rushed to catch him, but a pair of hands suddenly stopped me.

"Elyse? Elyse, is everything all right?"

I turned and looked to find John holding on to me.

"John?" I asked, blinking hard. "John? What are you doing here?"

He shook his head then smiled softly at me. "Perhaps you would not believe me if I told you. You look frightened, Elyse. What's wrong?"

The foreign gentleman was now out of sight. Where had he gone?

I sighed heavily. "It's Kai."

"Ah," John said, looking annoyed for a moment. "Then you must tell me all about it, but first, I have something I must ask you."

"Ask me?"

Then, quite unexpectedly, John took my hand and knelt on the ice before me.

"Miss Elyse McKenna, will you be my wife?"

17
NOTHING SOME FRATERNAL LOVE CAN'T FIX

I STARED AT JOHN. HE handed me a small clutch of yellow roses that I hadn't even noticed before then pulled a ring from his pocket. It was a small gold band. I stared at it then looked back at him. His honey-colored eyes shimmered in the morning sunlight.

John was grinning, but after a few moments passed, his smiled faded. "Elyse, you haven't said anything."

"Kai," I whispered, looking back over my shoulder toward the ship. Only the masts were still visible.

"Kai. Kai? Doctor Murray?" There was an edge to John's voice I had not heard before. That edge brought me back to the moment. John had proposed. John had just proposed. And in reply, I had said "Kai." At the mere thought of it, I burst out laughing. My overly-loud laugh echoed across the frozen river. I knelt and met John's eyes.

"Oh, my dearest. I think I've quite lost my mind. Please, please forgive me. It was just such a shock. I was distressed and…and, of course, I will marry you!"

John smiled, and reaching out, he slid off my glove. Moving carefully, he slipped the dainty gold ring on my finger.

The metal was cold against my skin. "It's beautiful. Oh, John," I whispered then threw myself at him, falling into his embrace. "I am so sorry," I said with a laugh.

"No, I am quite at fault. I…I wanted to ask you yesterday morning but I lost my nerve. I set my resolve this morning and came here with only one goal stubbornly in mind. As soon as I saw you, I knew I had to say it or I would lose my nerve again."

I giggled. "But why would you ever worry? You know that I care for you."

"Because…because when I asked you to marry me just now, you responded by speaking another man's name."

I balked. He was right. "Doctor Murray is like a brother to me. He is in trouble. My mind is in a fit over it."

John nodded. "And, because, perhaps it sounds silly, but I know many other fine gentlemen have tried for your attention, but you rebuked them. A beautiful and talented woman like you could have any man you wanted, no matter his station. Even Byron could not take his eyes from you."

"Byron cannot take his eyes off any woman. John, I would love you if you were a cobbler's son. It doesn't matter to me that you are Lord Waldegrave. To me, you are only John."

"Do you really mean that?" John exhaled so deeply that he shuddered.

"John?" I asked. He looked like he might be ill. Had his nerves been so awry?

"I...there is something more I must explain. My father's health is nearly spent. But I have learned something of his will," he said then reached out to touch my cheek. "He has written contingencies into the inheritance of his estate. Upon his death, I will take over his title only on the condition that I marry my cousin, Miss Harold."

I gasped.

"But if I am married before my father passes, this will void this condition of his will. I've met with my lawyer about the matter. He has confirmed it in light of the laws of heredity."

Something about this struck me as odd. The thought passed, however, when a new realization dawned on me. "Then we must wed at once."

John smiled brightly. "Yes. That's right. So, how does tonight suit you?"

"Tonight? I...please forgive me, I do understand the need for expedience, but I must make some arrangements. Do you think your father will last the week? I will need to arrange it with my company, and I need to acquire something proper to wear. And..." I said then paused. John's startling proposal had quite caught me off guard. More than ever,

I needed Kai's advice. How could I elope with Lord Waldegrave without Kai's opinion on the matter? And how could I just leave Kai in this state? No. It wasn't right.

"And there is the matter of your friend," John said with a sigh. For a brief moment, I saw him smother what appeared to be exasperation. He took a breath then said, "Very well, tell me what has happened."

I opened my mouth to speak, but suddenly the whole tale felt very silly. I was concerned because…because Kai had fallen into a liaison with an unseemly lover and was acting out of character. Kai, I had to remember, was a young, single man. How could I explain to John that it was more than just random carousing? Something was seriously wrong.

"You've met Doctor Murray. How would you describe his character?" I asked John.

"Dreadfully serious. Intellectual. Kind, of course, at least to you, but far too dour for my taste."

"Yes. That is him exactly. I'm afraid Doctor Murray has gotten himself caught up with Captain Behra, a lady captain on one of the ships frozen into the Thames. She and her crew are of the wildest sort, and if I didn't know better, I'd say she was holding him captive. I need someone to retrieve him. I went myself, but he was quite insensible."

"You mean disagreeable?"

"I mean drunk and, perhaps, under the influence of the poppy."

At that, John laughed. But when he saw the expression on my face he said, "You cannot be serious? Him? Why that's impossible."

"Yes. This was why I was so flustered. Really, Doctor Murray is the only person I have in this world. If we are to wed, even an elopement, I cannot leave without his blessing. And I certainly cannot leave him there in this condition. And now…what is the time?"

"Nearly nine."

"I'm supposed to be on stage in an hour!" My stomach quaked. Suddenly I felt like my world was turning upside down. So many different emotions washed over me. I was elated by John's proposal, furious with Captain Behra, or Tia, or whatever her name was, perplexed by and feeling annoyed with the baron, and still angry with Marion. And, above all, I was frightened for and upset with Kai. I sighed heavily.

"Tomorrow night will work fine, my love. I will make the arrangements for us, and you may settle your affairs. For now, please be at ease. But do keep your discretion in this matter. We can't have gossip reaching my family's ear before we are married."

"Of course," I said.

"Now, go prepare for your performance and don't worry. I shall chase Doctor Murray off the captain's ship. Nothing a stiff cup of coffee and a good kick in the arse won't fix."

I laughed out loud, surprised by his informality. "Really? You will do that for me?"

"Elyse, it has been clear to me from the start that you and Doctor

Murray are very close. I can see that he will always be a part of your life. And if he is like a brother to you, then he is a brother to me as well. And I know how to deal with a rowdy and out of sorts brother who is too deep in his cups and lost to the enchantments of a lovely woman."

"You really are too good to me."

"As I promise to be all your life. If you will have me, beggar that I am."

"With my body and soul."

"Promise?"

"I do."

John looked quickly around us. Seeing no one close by, he leaned in for a kiss. His lips brushed mine, and I caught the taste of anise in his mouth once more. "Now, go and play your Persephone. Put that wrinkled hag Marion to shame. Show them what my future wife is made of. As for me," he said, then nodded with his chin toward the ships.

"Thank you."

"Anything for you, my love," he whispered then kissed me on my forehead. "I'll come as soon as I have the issue settled for you."

Setting a kiss on my cheek once more, he turned and headed toward the ships.

I moved in the direction of the Ice House Theatre once more. Now, however, my heart was light. Of course, John would help me with Kai. Now, Kai would be safe, and I could revel in the fact that I was about to become a bride.

18
THE MOUSE

AS I MADE MY WAY back to the theatre, my heart beat hard in my chest. I'd stuffed my gloves into my pocket. I inhaled the perfume of the roses. Their sweet scent carried the smell of summer. As I walked, I twisted my ring around my finger. It felt so odd to be wearing it. I looked down, realizing that I hadn't even had a chance to examine it closely. The petite golden band shimmered an orange color in the morning sunlight.

My thoughts were disordered. But the further I walked, the deeper the realization came over me that tomorrow night, I would become Lady Waldegrave. John's father's will perplexed me. If the will stipulated that John should marry Miss-Whomever after his death, then what would happen when a marriage license was revealed dating before the death? John said his lawyer confirmed it would be all right. But did that make sense? I knew very little of the law. And if his estate did not pass to his only son, if there was some problem, then what would be done? John had no siblings...or did he? Now I wasn't sure. Regardless, tomorrow night, I would be wed. I would need to stop by the dressmaker and see if she could fashion me something suitable by tomorrow. I sighed a little, lamenting for just a fleeting moment the lack of a charming church wedding in Twickenham. But it didn't matter. What mattered was that I was going to wed the man I loved.

What also mattered was Kai. I had faith in John, and this matter seemed better handled between men. I could hardly tell if Kai was insensible or just being capricious. Had he been jealous of John and me? Was he acting this way just to get my attention? Did he know that the captain was married to the baron? Surely he knew that, right? If he was, indeed, amorous with her...well, I hardly knew what to make of it, but the idea of it filled me with loathsome anger.

Before I knew it, I had reached the Ice House Theatre once more.

"Elyse," Lizzie called the moment I stepped into the tent. She ran to the front of the tent and grabbed me by my arms. "Elyse, it's settled. I'm accepted at Saddler's Wells. I begin with their company next week. Can you believe it?"

Shaken from my thoughts, I smiled at the girl. I could hardly be jealous of her good fortune. A whole new future had just opened before me as well. "What wonderful news," I said then pulled her into a hug.

"How did Marve take the news?"

"Well, he was sad but also pleased for me. I think he fancies it is his job to nurture talent. And I think he is right. Oh, Elyse, surely you will be next. Are you playing Persephone this morning? When I came in, the ice was getting quite crowded. It was a bit warmer today so more people will be out."

"I am, but…" I said, unable to bite back the *but* before it slipped my lips.

"But?"

"May I borrow your ballet slippers? Titania's are too weak for Columbine, and I think mice got into mine."

"Mice?"

"Yes. Unfortunately, they got chewed, and I didn't have time to repair them properly last night."

Lizzie's eyes narrowed. "That's peculiar…about the mice."

"Foul rodents lurk everywhere," I said, looking toward Marion's section.

Lizzie's face hardened. "Indeed they are. Were those the slippers your grandmother gave you?"

"Sadly, yes," I said, then gave a cursory glance Marion's way. I could see her shadow against her partition. "They really were my most precious possession."

"Of course you can borrow mine. I'm so sorry, Elyse. If it is any comfort, rodents seem to always get what's coming to them."

"Thank you. I intend to throttle the creature to death if I ever get ahold of it. Such a heartless and vindictive little vermin."

At that, Marion's silhouette paused. For a moment, I imagined her like a shadow play. I envisioned a knight creeping up behind her and lopping off her head. The image of it playing through my mind gave me such intense glee I smiled.

"Let me get mine for you. I'll bring them in a moment," she said then rushed off.

I went then to my own section and pulled the Persephone costume from my trunk. It, at least, was still intact. It was always a joy to play in the comedia dell'arte. The comedia of Hades and Persephone was perfect for the Frost Fair and had, in truth, been my idea. Had the position of theatre manager not been prohibited to women, I often thought I would be very deft at the craft. But Isabelle Hawking had also inspired me. As Lady Waldegrave, I might have to give up acting, but I could certainly start my own ballet academy. There could hardly be any shame in teaching dance to young ladies. I mean, I hardly knew if such things were acceptable in higher circles, but I guessed they might be. Surely John's mother would guide me.

I shimmied out of my clothes and into the Persephone costume. It felt nice to wear a proper ballet costume. I then worked on my hair, pulling it back into a tight bun. Columbine's makeup was always very bright so I mellowed it some to give myself a more maidenly countenance. Given my pale cheeks, it only took a little makeup to do the job.

"Elyse, five minutes," Marve called from the front of the tent.

"Here you go," Lizzie said, appearing at the entrance of my section. She handed me her slippers.

"Thank you," I replied, smiling at her with gratitude.

"You should tell Marve," Lizzie whispered.

I shook my head. I was angry at Marion, but pitied her all the same. Like the rest of us, she had always dreamed of acting on a grand stage. For her, it was too late. Actresses never advanced after a certain age. She was jealous, and what she had done was cruel, but still, I could not hate her. After all, when my grandmother had died, Marion had sat with me and held my hand while I wept. That unexpected kindness had lodged itself in my memory.

Lizzie sighed. "You're too sweet, Elyse," she said with a soft smile then left.

Maybe she was right.

I finished off the last of the makeup, slipped my feet into my boots, then headed toward the stage, Lizzie's slippers in hand. I was delighted for the girl and couldn't wait to tell her my own news...the day after tomorrow.

As I turned the corner to exit the tent, I nearly ran into Marion.

"Elyse, I—" she began, but I pushed past her, saying nothing. Maybe I didn't want to ruin her over what she had done, but that didn't mean I forgave her. To destroy my slippers was a new low even for her.

I headed backstage. Sitting on a trunk, I pulled off my boots and slipped on the slippers. Marve stood watching as the final props were set up.

"Very good crowd, very good," he said then turned toward me. "Ah, here is the Persephone I know," he said with a smile, but then he paused. As I bent to tie up the laces on Lizzie's slippers, I felt Marve's eyes on me. "Elyse, did you get new slippers?"

"No."

"No?"

"These are Lizzie's slippers."

"What happened to the slippers your grandmother gave you?"

"Oh, just…a few stitches came loose, and I didn't have time to repair them. I'll work on them tonight and be ready for tomorrow morning. Marve, after the morning performance, may I have a word with you?"

"What about? Don't tell me you're leaving me for another troupe too."

I shook my head. "No, only a pressing obligation I must attend to tomorrow night."

"Very well," he said, "we can talk it over." He began rocking back and forth on his feet, a move I recognized well. He did it when he was nervous.

Hobbs, dressed as Harlequin, joined me backstage. "Ah, now, this will be a performance," he said, smiling at me. "Well, dear Persephone, are you ready to be snatched into the underworld?"

"I can't wait."

Playing the serious story of the abduction of Persephone as a comedy took a little skill. Since neither Hobbs nor I had more than ten lines in the entire skit, it was all in the delivery of the scene that made the set. While the commedia was stunningly simple to the viewer, to the artist, the face must express everything. I was glad to be playing across from Hobbs, who was a master at the pantomime.

A few moments later, Marve went out to welcome the audience, preparing the way for Hannah's brief prologue. I peered out the crack in the wall. The crowd was even larger than the night before. The sun was shining brightly. It was still very cold, but under such sun, surely the ice would begin to melt. I shook my head. I was still too lost in my own world, my own mind. I was still Elyse, and inside my head, names rattled around in circles—Kai, John, Captain Behra, the Baron, Kai, Marion, Kai— around and around they went.

I closed my eyes and squinted hard.

Silence!

Silence!

I inhaled deeply. I was not Elyse. I was the maiden of the spring setting out to pick some flowers. My life was nothing but joy and light.

And then Hades would come. First, he would woo with sweet words, and then he would woo with lies, and then he would try to ravish me, which I would cunningly avoid.

But before that, I was a simple, innocent girl.

The curtain lifted.

The strings on the harp sounded.

And on the tips of my toes, I pirouetted onto the stage.

19
THE MOUSE TRAP, PART I

HOBBS AND I WERE TAKING the final curtain call when we heard angry voices backstage. Over their applause and whistles, the audience would not have been able to hear, but I could distinctly make out Lizzie's, Marve's, and Marion's voices. Hobbs and I looked at one another out of the corner of our eyes, but our smiles never cracked. Hand in hand, we bowed once more and the curtain closed.

Hannah came out on stage to advise the audience of a ten-minute intermission before the story of *Glass Slipper Girl* began.

"What in the world?" Hobbs whispered to me as we both looked backstage. "Part of me is dying to know what the matter is. The other half of me is filled with dread."

"I couldn't have said it better," I agreed. Too curious to wait any longer, Hobbs and I headed back.

Outside the tent, Marve was shouting at Marion, his hand full of some odd bits of straw and string. Lizzie was holding my ballet slipper. Marion had turned an odd, ashen shade. She was so pale that I wondered if she was ill.

"What's happening?" Hobbs asked.

"Marion is leaving," Marve said then turned to me. He held out his hand. In it, intermingled with straw, I saw pink strings and a bit of silk. "Lizzie told me about your ballet slippers. I found this amongst the straw in Marion's section. It is very clearly from your slippers though Marion denies it."

"You cheap adder," Hobbs spat at Marion.

"There is no proof save a handful of string that could have fallen off any of our costumes," Marion retorted, but there was no heat behind her words.

Robert emerged from the tent and dropped a bag at Marion's feet. "That's all of it," he told Marve.

Marve nodded. "Leave. Now."

"Marve, I have been with this company for—"

"And all that time, jealous of every actress who has come and gone. But this is a new low, even for you. Do not even ask for a recommendation. I don't want to see or hear from you again."

Marion looked around at the assembled crowd, who was glowering at her. When her eyes rested on me, she sneered. "This is your fault," she hissed.

"My fault? Did I tell you to reward my kindness with ruining the single most important possession I own?"

"You have no proof!"

Marve threw the straw at her feet. "Leave. Now!"

Marion glared at me. "You will pay for this," she seethed then grabbed her bag and left.

For a moment, we all stood there, none of us breathing.

At the front of the theatre, a chime sounded. Five minutes until curtain.

"Good lord, I've forgotten all about the play. Elyse, can you play the role of the faerie godmother again?" Marve said.

I nodded. "Of course."

"Quickly then, get in costume. Let's just put this behind us for the moment, and we'll go for a pint afterward. We are professionals. Marion's unprofessional behavior cannot touch my troupe. Let's go out there and give them a great show," Marve said.

We all grinned at one another then dispersed.

I stopped by Marion's section and grabbed the faerie queen costume. As I exited the space, I looked down at the ground. There, just under the corner of a trunk, I spotted a scrap of pink ribbon. Part of me wondered if I had been paranoid, but the truth was evident enough. She had ruined my slippers. Well, it hardly mattered now. Marion was gone. The thought sent a wave of relief through my body.

I washed Persephone's makeup off then slipped on the silver faerie godmother costume. Digging through my trunk, I found an old silver wreath we'd used in a Christmas show. I didn't have enough time to redo my hair, but with just a few pins, I was able to affix the wreath and give myself an entirely different look. I then grabbed my wand and headed back toward the stage.

Marion was finally gone.

Good.

Justice had been served by those who loved me and were loyal to me. And they had also saved countless young actresses the burden of having to deal with her in the future. Despite the fact that Marion had, on occasion, treated me decently, it didn't excuse her petty behavior. I was sorry that she was unhappy, but it was not my fault. Marion had not settled into the parts of the middle-aged women with grace. It was too hard for her to let go the illusion of her own youth. And we had paid the price. But no more.

Rushing quickly, I found myself backstage once more.

The play had already begun, but my part was still some time away. I took my spot against the wall. As I did up the final ties on my gown, I looked out at the audience.

No John.

No Kai.

No baron. This was the first day he'd missed a performance. Perhaps the scolding from his wife had dulled his appetite for the theatre. That was a good thing. With their quarrel settled, the captain wouldn't have reason to toy with Kai any longer.

I frowned. Unless, of course, Kai wanted to be played with. No. He wasn't like that. I wouldn't have been surprised to see him become attached to Miss Hawking, but a lusty ship captain? No. That was too much.

All I could do was hope was that John had already taken Kai home and that Kai was in his own bed in his little garret apartment nursing a headache and a healthy sense of shame.

After all, Lady Justice was being very good to me today.

If only she could work for me a little longer.

20
THE MOUSE TRAP,
PART II

THE PERFORMANCE OF THE *GLASS Slipper Girl* seemed to fly by. When the show had ended, we all headed backstage to change.

"Elyse? Are you still going to come with us to the crowning?" Lizzie called from the opposite side of the tent.

"Crowning?"

"The Frostiana event, for the Frost Fair Queen," Amy answered.

"Say yes!" Hannah added.

"I thought we were going for a pint," Hobbs called from the gentleman's section.

The girls laughed.

"Stay out of this. We'll go after," Lizzie called. "Please, Elyse. Please come."

"Sure. I'll come." It had been an odd day. I started the morning in a fit of rage and fear, made a startling discovery about the baron, was now affianced and planning to elope, saw my nemesis fired, and now I was on my way to a Frost Fair Queen crowning.

The girls cheered.

"But we are going for a pint afterward," Hobbs insisted.

"Of course, of course," Lizzie called to him in reply. I could hear the smile in her voice.

A short while later, our troupe met at the front of the Ice House.

"Gentlemen," Marve said, turning to the men in our troupe, "the ladies will see about the Frost Fair Queen crowning, then they will join us at the City of Moscow for drinks. Lizzie was kind enough to permit us to go on ahead without them."

"Oh, Marve," she said, playfully squeezing his arm. "It's almost as if you don't want one of us to win a case of tripe."

Marve laughed.

At that, the gentlemen headed in one direction while the ladies headed in the other.

"Elyse," Lizzie said then, taking my arm. "Please forgive me for telling Marve about your slippers. I was so angry I couldn't control my tongue. Sweet and forgiving as you are, I knew you would never say anything. I had to bring the matter to Marve's attention. Marion, the witch, needed her due."

"Marion deserved what she got," Agnes said with stern authority. "I have been acting for thirty years, and I have never seen a less gracious performer in all my life. Add to that, she was not very good."

Everyone laughed.

I patted Lizzie's hand. "Don't apologize. I should thank you."

She smiled warmly at me.

"I do worry for Marve, though," Amy said. "If we are all hired off, he'll have no company left."

"I'm not going anywhere," Agnes said. "He'll always have a crone in the troupe. But this morning, all eyes were on Elyse. Was there a letter for you after this morning's show?" she asked.

In all of the excitement, I hadn't even thought of it. "No. I don't think so."

"No worries, my girl. Soon enough," Agnes said with authority.

"I don't know. Lately, I've been thinking of something new, something different, like a ballet academy for girls."

"An academy?" Lizzie asked excitedly. "That would be amazing."

"It would be a proper place for young women to study the craft, like the schools they have in Paris," I said.

Agnes nodded. "That is something much needed."

"Such a charming idea," Lizzie said. "And a very respectable trade," she added with a knowing wink. "Suitable for a lady," she whispered in my ear.

"Do you think so?" I asked her, my voice low.

"Absolutely."

I hoped she was right. And I also very much hoped to win over John's mother. I would be in desperate need of guidance once John and I were married. I knew that our marriage was not that desirable, but, perhaps, when they got to know me, when they learned of my character, John's family would change any pre-conceived notions they might have of actresses and see that I was a very sensible and moral young lady. Or so I hoped.

We turned off Freezeland Lane toward a section of the fair I had not yet visited. Here, someone had carved the massive sheets of ice jutting sideways out of the Thames into a frozen wonderland. Mermaids, water sprites, and seahorses had been carved as if they were arrested in motion, leaping from the magical kingdom below the ice. A strange ship with elaborate carvings sat trapped in the ice behind the display. In front of the ship where the ice had jammed, the artisans had chiseled a massive palace out of ice. Pillars carved into arching designs and faux stone walls surrounded two high thrones made of ice.

"It's nearly noon," Lizzie said. "Let's push through."

"I'll be fine right here," Agnes said, pausing to rest against a wine barrel.

Lizzie, Hannah, Amy, and I headed toward the front of the crowd. There, the tavern girls and shopkeeps, presumably the other contestants, waited for instruction. Their hair pulled back in neat coifs, lips stained red, looking as pretty as they could, they were ready for the competition.

"Maidens, maidens, gather around. Ladies, come this way," a merry lad in a bright blue coat said, motioning for the women to come forward. I noticed a familiar soft lilt in his voice, and his long yellow hair waved in the wind.

"Is that…" Lizzie asked, turning to me.

I looked the man over then shook my head. It was not the baron, though he looked very much like him.

Nearby, musicians played unusual stringed instruments. They rang silver bells, causing a sweet tune to carry across the ice. Someone had hung a garland of colorful cloths between the arches of ice.

A few moments later, the London marshall who was keeping watch over the Frost Fair came to the front of the crowd. From the red of his nose and cheeks, one could see he'd been deep in his cups.

"Ladies of the Frozen Fair," he said, his voice slurring. "Join us here in this palace of ice so we may delight in the treasures the Thames. We shall deliberate on your beauty, and in a few moments, your thoughts on this winter splendor. Our Frost Fair Prince, who has generously provided the awards for this debacle—debate—debut—pageant—will judge which maiden is the fairest in our frozen kingdom," the marshall called.

"How ridiculous," Hannah said with a snort.

"He's completely sauced," Lizzie added with a laugh.

"Doesn't matter. Come along, ladies. We have tripe to win," Hannah replied, pulling us into line with the other girls.

At that, we all laughed.

Lizzie, Hannah, Amy, and I joined the line of girls standing before the icy throne. When the ladies queued up, a cheer erupted from the crowd. The men called loudly when one of the tarts from The Frozen Mushroom lifted her coat to show off a very attractive leg.

"Come on, that's not fair," Lizzie called good-naturedly to her.

"Use what God gave you, marionette," the tart yelled back with a laugh.

"She has knobby knees anyway," Lizzie told me.

"I suspect it wasn't her knees they were looking at. Her arse was half-hanging out," Amy replied.

I giggled. Hannah was right. This was ridiculous. No one seemed to know what was going on. Regardless, we ladies waited patiently for the pageant.

I scanned over the crowd as the marshall and the strangers finished organizing the ladies. Quite a throng had assembled. I recognized many of them as attendees at the Ice House Theatre. It seemed like the audience on the ice simply moved from wonder to wonder.

And the scene around me was, in fact, a wonder. The artisans had carved an elaborate castle. The sharp contrasts of crystalline ice shot with flecks of blue, glowing golden on the edges under the sun, was a sight to behold. On the upper peak, someone had carved a dragon clutching the roof of the castle. I couldn't help but notice the water dripping off its wing as the sun beat down on the fierce creature.

Movement on the ship behind me caught my attention. A moment later, three men made their way from the ship, through the ice palace, to the judging area where we ladies waited.

"And here is our Frost Fair Prince," the marshall called.

Rather than a blast of trumpets, a lovely chime announced their arrival. Two of the men, each of whom carried wooden chests, held back to allow the third man, in his fine blue suit trimmed with ermine, walking with his cane, to come forward. His pale yellow hair shimmered almost incandescently surrounded by the icy palace of wonders. He turned to the crowd and bowed. Then he turned to us and made a similar bow. After that, he sat down on his throne of ice.

I locked my eyes on the baron.

When he met my gaze, he smiled.

My expression went hard.

In return, a look of worry crossed his face.

"Elyse?" Lizzie whispered, looking at me. "What's wrong?"

"Nothing," I replied. Remembering myself, I pulled on a serenely sweet false face. Lady MacBeth could not have done better.

The baron's surprised expression eased, but I saw his forehead furrow with confusion.

I looked away.

"Now, ladies, let us begin. As I come around, please tell us your names and give us a spin so we may observe your finery," the marshall called with a naughty laugh, raising and lowering his eyebrows.

"Finery, indeed!" Hannah said with a giggle.

At the sound of a gong, we began.

First, there was Elizabeth. The buxom girl, who I'd seen at the fishmonger's tent, stepped forward and curtseyed first to the foreign gentleman and then to the crowd. "My name is Elizabeth Adams," she said. Taking her skirt by her fingertips, she bowed to the crowd, giving her ample bosom a shake.

"She's about to pop out," Lizzie whispered.

"Then she'll win for sure," Hannah added, causing us all to suppress a laugh.

The crowd roared with delight.

The baron merely smiled, nodded to her, then motioned with just the slightest gesture of his hand for the next woman to come forward.

There was Daphne, Lara, Mary, Claudia, another Mary, Beth, Charlotte, Rosie—the girl who'd shown her leg—Katie, Poppy, Penny, Jane, and Frances. In turn, each lady had stepped forward, shared her name, and gave the loveliest, or bawdiest, turn. Rosie, who introduced herself as a tart from The Frozen Mushroom, treated the audience with a shimmy of her backside, and *accidently* exposed her knickers, as she showed off her finery.

As she clowned, I glanced at the baron. He had a slightly bored expression on his face. His eyes darted toward me, and he raised an eyebrow. The sudden expression of concern melted my anger. After all, it was not his fault that his wife was a jealous whore. In fact, more was the pity. Nor was it my fault that Kai decided to run amok. I was simply an actress, and like so many others, the baron was simply an admirer. Captain Behra *was* a very jealous and petty woman. The quarrel was not between the baron and me. I had no right to be angry with him. And more, with John's help, the problem was done. By now, John had pumped Kai full of coffee and good advice.

I smiled softly at the baron then turned my attention to the marshall. He'd finally reached us.

"Come along, young lady," he said, motioning to me. This close, I could smell the stench of wine wafting off him.

Even before I said a word, the audience broke into applause.

"Titania! Titania!" several people in the audience called.

I smiled and dropped a nice curtsey. Once they fell silent, I turned to the crowd and put on my best smile. "I see I am known to many of you as Titania. We are all players at the Ice House Theatre, the temporary home for the players at Struthers Theatre," I said, motioning to my friends. "While I play Titania, my real name is Elyse McKenna."

Moving carefully in my winter boots, I took my long skirts in one hand, and raised my other arm above me in the most graceful pose I could, bending with the arch, and then moving deftly, I gave the crowd the nicest fouetté spin I could manage in winter boots and a long coat.

A hush fell over the crowd for a moment and then they broke into a cheer.

"A case of tripe for Elyse for sure," Amy said with a laugh.

"Show off," Rosie called, sticking her tongue out at me.

I bowed to her, winking playfully, then stepped back in line. My eyes quickly darted to the baron who nodded to me.

After me, Lizzie was introduced.

"Cinderella! Cinderella!" the audience called.

I smiled, pleased for Lizzie that she too was so well-recognized. Lizzie made her introduction with Amy and Hannah following thereafter.

"What lovely, lovely girls. Such finery as the Thames has never seen before. Wouldn't you agree?" the marshall called.

The crowd cheered.

"Now, ladies, before we have a final judging, let's see how well you can answer a question. Your lordship," the marshall said, turning to the baron.

"Ladies, let us hear your thoughts," he said, leaning forward on his walking stick that was braced between his legs. "Describe for us the wonder of the frozen Thames. Give us your verses."

Once more, the marshall worked his way down the lines.

Elizabeth said, "The Thames has been transformed to mountains of frozen cream."

"Tasty image," Lizzie said as she clapped.

"Fish-flavored ice cream?" Hannah asked.

"The Thames is shimmering like the clouds of heaven," Daphne, a tavern wench at The Frozen Mermaid, said.

"Not bad, not bad," Lizzie said, clapping.

"Nice turn of a line," Amy agreed.

"The Thames may be hard as a woman's nipples on a winter's morning, but she'll still soften to a man's warm touch," Rosie said, earning her a loud cheer and boisterous laughter.

We clapped loudly.

"Clever tart," Hannah said, whooping for her.

Lizzie stuck her fingers in her mouth and let out a whistle of approval.

I looked at the baron. Even he was chuckling at that one.

On down the row they went until it was my turn.

"And you, Titania?" the marshall asked when he came to me once more.

I looked up toward the melting dragon. "I say jealous winter froze the Thames so she could play faerie games upon its surface. Frosty but kind, she will stay until she's soothed to peace by the loving sun."

A round of heavy applause rewarded my line. I felt pleased with myself, yet at the same time, a strange emptiness washed over me. It had been a nice line, and Kai had not been there to hear it. The hollowness I felt at his absence disquieted me. Shouldn't I have thought of John?

The marshall turned to Lizzie. "And you, Cinderella?"

Lizzie grinned and in her stage voice, she pronounced, "Now is the winter of my discontent…my discontent that it's still winter," she said, playing with Shakespeare's famous lines.

Recognizing the turn of phrase, several people in the audience laughed and cheered for her. Amy and Hannah followed Lizzie.

"Now, ladies and gentlemen, let's bring forth the Frost Fair Prince to rule over the judging."

At that, the baron rose. His two attendants also came forward carrying the chests.

He walked down the line, smiling at each girl in turn as she gave him a polite curtsey. When he reached me, he met my eyes. He smiled softly at me then moved past. Lizzie jabbed me in the ribs with her elbow. Then, in his role as Frost Fair Prince, the baron went back to the front of the crowd.

"What is the best measure of beauty?" he asked the crowd.

They flung a variety of answers at him, from nice legs to a round arse to a pretty face to a good cook.

Smiling, he lifted his cane to silence them. "You are right, my friends, that a fair face is a thing to behold. And, true, that a nice round bottom is a pleasure on a warm night. Loyalty, honesty, and warmth of heart are, I say, worth far more than these. But that, my friends, is the most difficult to see.

"I have three prizes to share today. The first prize goes to she is who is fair of face. I call Lizzie Montgomery, your Cinderella, to claim her prize. Was there ever a lady fairer than the princess of the glass slipper?"

At that, the crowd cheered wildly.

The baron motioned for one of his men to step forward while he also beckoned to Lizzie.

We cheered our friend on as she went to collect her prize. I suppressed the sharp pang of jealousy that tripped at my breast. Lizzie really was pretty, and she had a lightness and sweetness of spirit that radiated from inside her. I reminded myself to be pleased for her.

The baron opened one of the chests. From inside, he pulled out a small object. He lifted it for everyone to see. On a bright red ribbon hung a crystal snowflake pendant. It shimmered in the sunlight, casting blobs of rainbows around the crowd.

The crowd cheered excitedly.

Moving carefully, he slipped it over Lizzie's neck then bowed to her in congratulations.

One of the baron's attending gentlemen took Lizzie by the arm and led her to stand with him near the thrones of ice.

The baron turned back to the crowd. "Beauty also lies in the flesh. The warmth of a woman's skin, the softness of her lips, and the lustiness of her eyes are all treasures to behold," he said then smiled. "I do believe fair Rosie from The Frozen Mushroom must have this prize."

Whistles and applause sprang from the crowd.

The baron motioned for a second chest to be opened. From inside, he pulled forth a hair comb made of silver and trimmed with flowers and sparkling gems. He gently slid the comb into the tart's hair. A hush seemed to fall over Rosie's spirit as she was awarded such a fine thing. It glimmered in her dark hair, a thing of pure goodness that seemed to cast its glow onto the wearer.

The baron leaned forward, whispering something in her ear.

To my surprise, Rosie blushed.

She curtseyed to him, and then his attendant led her to join Lizzie.

"Ah, gentlemen, it is hard to find a woman who has pure beauty and a pure heart, isn't it? Such rare queens are a true treasure. But there is one lady here who surpasses all the rest. She is the loveliest, warmest of heart, and the most elegant creature I have *ever* seen. Miss Elyse McKenna, come forward and be my queen."

The crowd broke into elated cheers and applause.

While the wildness and excitement of the crowd impressed itself upon me, I couldn't help but take a second to ruminate on his words. Given the nature of his quarrel with his wife, selecting me his queen was most certainly going to annoy Captain Behra even more. Add that to John taking Kai from her clutches, I strongly suspected the captain was going to be very unhappy with me.

Regardless, I moved forward, joining the baron. "For the Frost Fair Queen." From within his jacket, he pulled out a magnificent silver hand mirror. The piece, elaborately crafted, was a thing of beauty. The mirror was no larger around than my palm, but the back of the mirror and all the edges had been trimmed in silverwork like I'd never seen before. Images of nymphs and satyrs, vines, flowers, and birds trimmed the mirror.

"In case the wind ever plays with your hair again, you'll have this on hand," he said in a low voice.

I looked up at him. The prize was too perfect. How had he known I would come? Had he intended this for me all along?

"Thank you," I whispered.

"There is more to this mirror than meets the eye, but first, do come," he said, offering me his arm.

As the crowd cheered, the baron led me to the thrones of ice.

"Ladies and gentlemen of the Thames, may I introduce your King and Queen!" the London marshall called.

At that, the crowd erupted into a cheer.

From behind me, one of the attendants set a ring of Frost Fair roses on my head, and the baron and I sunk into our seats.

A moment later, however, there was a sharp cracking sound.

The crowd stilled.

The wind blew harshly, and the sun was occluded as dark clouds moved in. Thunder rolled and lightning cracked.

"What was that? Is the ice cracking?" someone asked, their voice lifting above the dead silence of the crowd.

We were all frozen as we listened. A moment later, there was a terrible cracking sound, and the ice below our feet trembled. Everyone stood still, gripped by fear as a crack appeared in the ice under the crowd's feet. Gasping, they backed away in horror as they watched the long crack travel the length of the Thames like a vase that has been nicked on its edge but not shattered.

"Sunny morning," the London marshall called out with a nervous laugh. "No doubt the Thames is getting ready to take the river back. My friends, one more round of applause for our king and queen then go on and enjoy and be merry. I fear the Frost Fair may be reaching its end."

I turned to look at the baron who had an odd expression on his face. He was looking in the direction of Captain Behra's ship. After a moment, he turned and looked at me.

"Miss McKenna, I am sorry, but I must leave you now. I have a matter I must attend to. I may have overplayed a hand and need to ensure no one gets hurt."

"Of course," I said, rising.

Already, the crowd at the fair began to disperse, worried conversations springing up amongst the revelers as to how long the ice was going to hold.

"But wait…the mirror. You said—"

The baron was motioning to his attendants to join him.

"Ah, yes, the mirror. I did select it especially for you," he said with a smile. "A special gift for a very special woman."

I was right. "I…" I began, but I didn't know what to say.

"Say nothing. It has been many years since I've met a woman as fair as you. You remind me of someone…in better days. As for the mirror, it will keep your hair in order but also do much more. Under the light of the moon, all your heart's desires will be revealed," he said then bowed to me. "I'm sorry, I must be going."

At that, he waved to the others and the three of them departed in the direction of Captain Behra's ship.

"Elyse! Congratulations! Oh, let me see," Lizzie said, joining me.

"A hand mirror," I told her.

"It's beautiful. And look at this," she added.

I admired the snowflake necklace. It shimmered with a rainbow of light. It was so beautiful. As I stared at it, I found myself momentarily lost, thinking once more of the ballet academy I wished to create.

"You know," Lizzie said, interrupting my thoughts, "this lovely thing has given me some ideas of how we should change tonight's performance. I was thinking, I've been throwing Hermia's lines all wrong. I suspect I never fully appreciated Master Shakespeare's character, but it just struck me that Hermia is actually to be pitied," she began, her voice trailing off as she talked over her new interpretation of the Bard's work.

I turned from her for just a moment, my eyes following the baron as he receded through the crowd.

"Lizzie. Elyse. I'm very disappointed," Agnes called as she approached.

"Agnes?"

"What? No tripe?"

At that, Amy and Hannah, who had also joined us, laughed.

"No, but we'd better get the Frost Fair Queen over to the City of Moscow for a pint with the boys before they give up on us," Hannah said.

"May we see?" Amy asked, looking at the mirror.

I handed it to her.

"Oh, it's magnificent," Agnes breathed.

I turned my attention from them to find that Rosie, the tart, had taken off her hair comb and was sitting on the ice throne, turning the piece around in her hand.

"Excuse me for a moment," I said then went to her. "Rosie, I just wanted to offer my congratulations."

She looked up at me. Her dark eyes were brimming with unshed tears. "It's so lovely, isn't it?" she said then turned her eyes to the comb once more. Her expression unguarded, I could see how truly pretty she was under all the makeup and pretense of a whore.

"It is. Truly pretty."

She frowned then looked up at me. "Elyse, right?"

I nodded.

"I need some money."

I cocked my head and looked at her.

A single tear rolled down her cheek. "I want to go home."

I reached into my small purse to give her some of the coins I carried but then thought better of it. I handed my purse to her. "Then go home," I told her.

"Thank you," she said. She took my purse, slipped it inside her coat, reaffixed the comb in her hair, and then turned and headed away from the Frost Fair toward the city.

"Elyse? Are you ready?" Amy called.

I turned back to my friends, pausing for just a moment to watch Rosie walk away, her hair comb glimmering brightly under the scant rays of sunlight that fought their way through the dark clouds.

21
OF GREEN JACKETS

THE TAVERN ON THE ICE, dubbed the City of Moscow, was completely packed. It seemed like all the patrons had come for a pint and a bit of bread and cheese.

There was barely space to sit when we finally found Robert, Hobbs, Marve, James, and Skippy.

"What, no case of tripe?" Robert called as we approached.

Skippy immediately ran off to procure more chairs, and the other gentlemen moved to make space for us.

"Lizzie and Elyse both won prizes," Agnes said.

"And Elyse is the Frost Fair Queen," Lizzie said very loudly, causing the other patrons to turn and look.

Upon seeing the crown of Frost Fair roses I wore and ruminating on

Lizzie's words, the crowd put the two together and let out a cheer.

I smiled and waved then sat down. What an odd, odd day. I was beginning to wonder what else could possibly happen. At this rate, I'd be having tea with the real queen by late afternoon.

The gentlemen congratulated me, and soon I found myself holding a mug of mulled wine. I took a sip, letting the hot, spicy wine warm my body, then set the mug down.

"Did you hear that crack in the ice?" Amy asked the gentlemen.

"I'm going to have the wagon brought around and load up the first of our belongings tonight. Tomorrow, we'll perform on a bare stage," Marve said.

"If there is a stage by morning," Hobbs added.

"It's still cold," Agnes said. "The ice will refreeze overnight."

"True, it is cold, but not as chilled as it has been," Robert replied.

"Such a pity," Lizzie lamented. "The fair has been a treat. I hate to see it end."

"No doubt the marshalls will have us off the ice if it begins to weaken along the edges," Marve said. "But just in case, we'll be cautious. With the crowd we gather, all that weight, we must be wary."

The others nodded then fell further into the discussion.

I leaned back in my seat and surveyed the space, looking for a young man in a green coat. My eyes had played tricks on me the day Lizzie and I had come for the Frost Fair handbill. As I looked around the room, I noticed several young men of John's build in green coats. I was a very silly girl. How could I think so badly of him?

"Marve," I said, touching his arm. "I had meant to tell you that I will not be able to perform in *Midwinter* tomorrow night."

"No?" he said, raising an eyebrow. "Is something wrong?"

In that moment, I realized I had not come up with a suitable excuse. "I…my friends, the Hawkings, are having some problems and need help. I told them I would see if I would be missed."

"Of course you will be missed," he said with a smile. "But Hannah can take your role for the night."

Lizzie was listening with interest. "Is everything all right?"

I nodded, choking the telling expression that wanted to creep up on my face.

Lizzie raised an eyebrow at me.

I looked away from her, realizing she knew me far too well.

"Miss McKenna?" someone asked from behind me.

I turned to find one of the Frost Fair pamphlet makers standing behind me. I recognized him from the booth, as if his ink-stained smock was not telling enough.

"Yes?"

"I'm sorry to bother you, Miss. Someone told me you were here. Would I be able to steal a few minutes of your time? We would very much like to have your autograph on the Frostiana announcements. It is too much to ask, I know, but your signature would add value to the papers.

Now that the event is over, and the ice is beginning to soften, it's our last chance to sell," the man said as he awkwardly rubbed the back of his neck.

I smiled softly at him. "Certainly. I'll be back in ten minutes," I told the others.

"Farewell, your Majesty," Lizzie called with a laugh.

I followed the man outside.

"Thank you, Miss," he said, leading me to his tent. "I was afraid we'd lose our investment on those flyers, but the autograph of the Frost Fair Queen will sell."

"A queen can do no less than aid her subjects," I said with a laugh.

He grinned. "No wonder people say such nice things about you, Miss McKenna, you and Doctor Murray. Everyone knows how you both worked to save that man from the ice. How is he, anyway?"

"Recovering very well."

The other two men inside the tent rose when I entered.

"Told you she would come," the man at my side said. "I'm Tom, by the way. And that's Nick and Peter," he said, pointing to the men.

"Well, hand me a stack, gentlemen," I said, pulling off my gloves.

Taking a seat by their brazier, I settled in and began signing, *Elyse McKenna, Frostiana, Frost Fair Queen, 1814* on the flyers. The men joked merrily as they worked on their prints. After I finished the first handful, Tom went out front and began barking down the lane:

"Frost Fair handbills! Get your Frost Fair handbills signed by

Frostiana, our Frost Fair Queen, the talented Elyse McKenna."

To my surprise, a crowd gathered to purchase the papers.

I worked busily, signing paper after paper. On occasion, I would smile and wave to the crowd. It was funny how I had achieved instant celebrity status. I had been there at least half an hour when I looked up once more, fully expecting to see Lizzie and Marve, but then I spotted yet another young man in a green jacket. He was purchasing hot chocolate for a pretty, and very giggly, young woman in a red bonnet. The crowd milled between us, obscuring my view, but the cut of the young man looked so much like John that it fully took up my attention. When the crowd moved on, I leaned in my seat to look once more. The young man's back was toward me. He pulled off the lady's glove and kissed her hand before handing her a mug of hot chocolate. She blushed and giggled once more. When he returned her glove, he leaned in and put a kiss on her cheek. He then turned to put on his top hat. And in that moment, I got a good look at him.

John? I stood. "John?" I called. My stomach felt like it had fallen to my feet.

The man turned toward the sound of my voice. When he met my eyes, the expression on his face fell flat, and he quickly turned away. The crowd moved in between us.

"There she is. Elyse," I heard Lizzie call from the crowd. "We need to go, love."

I rose, trying to get a better look at the man…at John. This time, I was certain it was him.

"Miss?" Peter asked.

"Gentlemen, I am very sorry. I need to go," I said. I bit my lip. My hands were shaking. Was it him? Had it really been him? Who was that girl?

"Thank you for your time, Miss McKenna. We're very grateful," Peter told me. "Tom, Miss McKenna needs to leave," he called to his friend.

"One moment, people, one moment," Tom called to the crowd.

I was already moving toward the chocolate vendor when Tom intercepted me.

"You all right, Miss McKenna?" Tom asked.

"Yes. Fine. I...I left you a healthy stack on the table. I do hope my signature fetches you some coin," I told him and with a nod, I moved through the crowd toward the chocolate vendor. My heart beating hard in my chest, I looked frantically around for John and that girl. There was no one. They were gone.

Lizzie came up to me. "What's wrong?"

"Lizzie," I said, taking her by the arm. "Did you see Joh—Lord Waldegrave?"

She looked confused. "No, I don't think so."

"There," I said, pointing to the chocolate stand, "with a woman in a red bonnet."

She frowned hard. For the second time that day, her face flushed with anger. "No, I did not. I would certainly say so if I had...right after I smacked him in the face. Was it him? Are you certain?"

"I think so. Yes, I'm certain. He was there with a lady in a red bonnet."

Lizzie and I both looked around the crowd. There was no one nearby wearing red.

"Maybe…maybe she was a friend?" Lizzie offered.

"No. He kissed her cheek in a tender way, like a lover."

"Then it wasn't him. He's devoted to you, Elyse. I'm sure of it."

I slipped off my glove and showed her my hand. "Tomorrow night. We're planning to elope tomorrow night."

"Then it wasn't him. The crowd is large. It was not him."

And if it was? If it was John, then he was not with Kai. That could mean Kai was still in danger.

"When are you planning to see him again?" Lizzie asked.

"I…I'm not sure."

"Then send word for him to come meet you."

"I cannot."

"Why not?"

"His family…his father is very ill, and I don't exactly know where he is staying."

"You don't know where he is staying?" Lizzie asked, her eyes narrowing. She fingered the crystal pendant she was wearing. "Doesn't that strike you as odd, especially if you are intended to be his wife?"

"I know his estate is in Twickenham. He's just in London for a short while because his father is ill."

"If his father is ill, why is he here in London and not at their estate? Waldegrave...aren't the Waldegraves connected to Smallbridge Hall in Suffolk? My grandmother lived not far—"

"Oh no, he said his estate is in Twickenham. It was inherited from Lord Walpole."

Lizzie's forehead furrowed as she thought it over. She shook her head. "I confess, I don't know. Such people are like the stars above us. Only Lord Byron bothers to roll around at our level," she said with a laugh. Despite my upset mood, I couldn't help but smile.

"Roll around, eh?" I asked.

Lizzie's cheeks burned very red very quickly. "I, um, well. Marve said we need to get back. We need to pack up our supplies before the performance. Please don't worry. If he loves you enough to wed you, then all is well. Just...just ask him and measure his honesty with an open mind."

"As you measured Byron's?"

Lizzie laughed. "That man has no honesty. At least, not with me. Perhaps not with anyone."

"Oh, someday he'll meet his match. Men like that always do. But tell me, does he roll around well?"

"The best," she said wistfully.

I sighed, my thoughts momentarily drifting to the handsome poet. "So I imagined."

Lizzie laughed, and at that, I set my worries aside. No. It could not have been John. It wasn't possible. It just wasn't possible. No one who truly loved me could ever betray me like that. John had done as he'd promised. He'd gotten Kai safely home. All would be well.

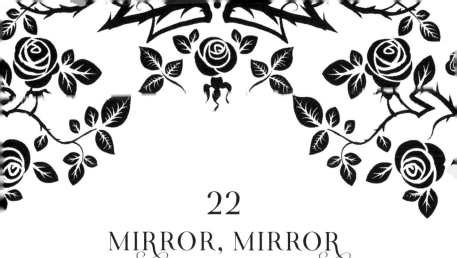

22
MIRROR, MIRROR

BACK AT THE ICE HOUSE, we worked busily packing up our belongings. Skippy brought the wagon from the theatre, and we soon began stripping anything of value. If the Thames reclaimed the river overnight, she would not take all of Struthers Theatre's hard-won belongings with it. I stuffed the Persephone costume into my bag then quickly dressed as Titania as I prepared for the evening performance.

The crowd that gathered outside that night was much smaller than it had been the night before. From the number of wagons going back and forth between the river and the city, it was clear that crack in the ice had made people nervous. From my spot backstage, peering through the theatre entrance, I saw that at least two of the tents that had been across from the theatre were now gone.

"Thinning out," Marve said as we peered through the slats.

"They're frightened."

"It's cold tonight, though. Colder than last night, I think."

I nodded.

I scanned the crowd. No Kai. No John. Not even the baron was there.

Onstage, Hermia pleaded with Theseus for the right to marry the man she truly loved.

I frowned. Where was John? For that matter, where was Kai? I was impatient for the play to be done. I wanted to go home and talk to Kai. He had a lot of explaining to do, and I desperately needed his advice. What if I *had* seen John today? I bit my lip and tried to rein in my frustrations. I would channel them to Titania.

Hermia's scene ended, and I took to the stage.

"Ill met by moonlight, proud Titania," Robert called.

"What, jealous Oberon?" I retorted bitterly, loving him and hating him all at once. I looked back to Hannah and the others who were dressed as faeries. "Faeries, skip away. I have forsworn his love and company."

"Rash woman. Aren't I your lord?"

"Then I must be your lady."

Once more, Master Shakespeare took control. Letting my anger and frustration roll out of me through Titania's lines, I diced Oberon with my words until he turned the tables on me, making me fall in love with a man who was an ass.

Before I knew it, the play was done and once more I was backstage listening as Anderson delivered Puck's final words. I mouthed my favorite lines along with him. "If we shadows have offended, think but this and all is mended, that you have but slumbered here while these visions did appear."

Finally, curtain call came.

While the others were in a jovial mood, I couldn't wait to leave.

"Elyse, want to come for dinner?" Lizzie asked me. I could see by the expression on her face that she knew something was wrong.

"No, thank you. It's been a long and very odd day. I'm going to stop by the Hawkings' then head home. I think I need some sleep."

"All right," she said with a careful smile. "We'll see you in the morning."

I nodded then went back out into the night. The river was much quieter than it had been the evening before. The families and fine ladies and gentlemen were notably absent. Debauchery was in full swing, but the better class of people had gone. I eyed the masts of Captain Behra's ship as I made my way off the ice. Her lanterns were still burning brightly. My stomach flopped. But I reminded myself that it didn't matter. She could be annoyed with me as much as she wanted. As long as Kai was out of her grasp, I didn't care if she was jealous and angry with her husband. That was her problem. I was an innocent. How was I to know he was married? How was I to know he was the Frost Fair Prince? Surely she could not begrudge me that.

I felt at my inside pocket. The mirror was still there. Later tonight, I would test it, see what moonlit enchantment it held. Part of me fancied that it would really work, but there was no such thing as magic.

I turned in the direction of the Hawkings' workshop. As I went, I realized I had not done as I had originally planned and gone to the millinery between shows. I had no dress to wear tomorrow night. I sighed heavily. How could I forget such a thing? I would go first thing in the morning before I returned to the Ice House.

As I neared the Hawkings' workshop, I slowed. The house was dark. That was odd. It was not late. Surely they would still be awake. Maybe Master Hawking and Isabelle were out. I could still stop and see the gentleman.

I knocked on the door.

A few moments later, the footman opened it. "Miss McKenna," he said nicely. "I'm very sorry, but the master and Miss Isabelle are not in."

"Oh, I'm sorry to hear it. Perhaps…perhaps I can see Doctor Murray's patient if he is still awake."

At that, the servant smiled. "Ah, we have good news there and the very reason the Hawkings are out. The gentleman recovered his memory. Master Hawking and Miss Isabelle went with him to the Bow Street Runners and to meet with the gentleman's family."

"Oh, that is good news. Well then, I'll be sure to stop in the morning."

"Very good, Miss McKenna. I'll be sure to let Master Hawking know you were by. Goodnight," he said and moved to close the door.

"I'm sorry, just one more question. Was Doctor Murray here today?"

"Doctor Murray?"

"Yes?"

"I'm sorry, we haven't seen him today."

"Not at all?"

"No, Miss McKenna."

"Very well. Thank you very much."

He nodded then closed the door.

My mind lost in the circus of confusion that surrounded me, I hurried home. At least it was good news that the gentleman was well. I would have to inquire again and see if I could learn his real name and the circumstances that found him in the river. The matter set aside for the moment, I turned and headed home. All my thoughts bent on Kai. I had no right to begrudge him a fling with a foreign beauty. After all, I didn't own him in any way save the familial love between us. But still. He had no right to make me worry, and it wasn't right for him to have a liaison with a married woman.

When I reached the front door of my home, I looked up. I could not see our garret windows from the ground. I hastily let myself inside and raced up the steps. Panting and out of breath, I flung open the door of my flat hoping the light would be on and the fire lit, a guilt-ridden Kai sitting at my table nursing a headache. But the room was cold and dark.

I swung the door shut behind me and rushed to the window, drawing back the curtains. A waft of cold air rolled off the glass window pane. The

Frost Fair roses Kai had given me sat wilted in the vase. Kai's window was dark. I opened the latch. Crawling out, I stepped carefully across the roof to Kai's window and opened it.

I looked inside to find the loft was entirely dark and freezing cold.

"Kai?" I whispered into the darkness.

There was no answer.

Frowning, I closed the window then sat down on the roof between our garrets. The flower pots between the windows sat empty, the dead plants clinging lifelessly to the sides. I looked up at the sky. The moon was shining. How many summer nights had Kai and I spread out a blanket on the roof and lay looking at the stars? And before it was just the two of us, our grandmothers sat with us, giving us lemonade and sweets as we watched the moon drift across the night's sky. And now, where was Kai?

I stared at the moon. And then I remembered the baron's gift.

I pulled the mirror from my pocket. I looked into it, seeing a look on my face that I didn't recognize. I looked very sad. "Why so sad, Elyse? You'll be Lady Waldegrave by tomorrow night."

As the moonlight shimmered down onto the mirror, the sparkling silver took on a strange hue. The looking glass glowed with a blue light.

"Isn't that what you want, Lady Waldegrave?" I whispered to myself then looked back at Kai's dark window.

I looked once more into the mirror. The image therein surprised me. I saw myself, smiling as if the sun shone down on me. For a moment, the image fogged and a hand appeared on my shoulder, another face coming into frame behind me. Kai set a sweet kiss on my bare neck before he looked up at me through the mirror and smiled.

Yelping, I dropped the mirror into my lap.

My hands trembled.

I squeezed my eyes closed and drowned out the voice inside me that yelled things that did not make sense. I loved John. Surely I did. I loved him, didn't I? But if I did, if I truly did, then why could I not shake the sense that my affection for John was nothing more than a whim, no stronger than Kai's attraction to the captain? If I truly loved him, why couldn't I shake the sense that marrying John would cost me the one thing I valued the most? Kai.

Moving carefully, I picked up the mirror and slipped it back into my pocket. I didn't dare look at again. I went back inside my garret apartment and locked the window behind me. I lay down on my bed, sliding the mirror under my pillow. I could hear Granny nagging at me to remove my coat and boots, but I couldn't get up. I closed my eyes, feeling the tears prick at the corners. The hot tears slid down my cheeks, and sobs followed. I wept so hard my body shook.

I groaned then clutched the blankets with my hands, squeezing them into fists.

"Kai, where are you?"

23
LORD JOHN WALDEGRAVE

I WOKE THE NEXT MORNING in the hope that Kai had returned during the night, but still, his window was dark. Had John failed to retrieve him? Was he ill? Hurt? Had Kai sent John away, preferring to stay with the captain? A dark mood fell over me as I considered that the captain's jealousness might cause her to do something rash. Surely, I was being paranoid.

In a wretched mood, I dressed and headed back to the river. My stomach felt like someone had tied it into knots. I needed to do something. Things couldn't drag on like this with me not knowing what had befallen Kai, even if it was just a lusty interlude.

When I arrived at the Ice House Theatre, I found that the backstage tent had been stripped down to her bare bones. The wagon waited outside so it could be loaded at the first warning that the Frost Fair was done. Inside the tent, I heard the voices of my fellow players as they prepared for the morning show.

I went to my section and began preparing for the morning pantomime. I slipped on Persephone's costume then worked on fixing my hair.

I knew I should feel excited, but I could not. Instead, I felt frightened. I was supposed to get married tonight, to elope with a man I loved. It was everything a girl like me should have wanted. But if so, why did I feel so sad?

I picked up the makeup brush to line my eyes when Marve called me.

"Elyse? Are you in yet?"

"Yes, I'm here."

A moment later, Marve arrived at my partition. I could see his shadow on the other side of the dressing screen as he hesitated.

"I'm dressed."

Marve chuckled then turned the corner. "Ah, yes. Here is Persephone. You were so quiet this morning that I thought you were running late."

I gave him a half-smile.

"What's the matter?" Marve asked, his forehead furrowing.

I shook my head. "It's nothing."

"My dear, you have been in my company for five years. Don't tell me it's nothing."

"I'm all right, just distracted."

Marve nodded then began rocking back and forth on his heels. "Well, perhaps this will cheer you. A gentleman in the audience asked me to send you this before the performance," he said then handed me a box.

"A gentleman?"

Marve nodded. "He said there is a note inside."

"What's in it?" I asked.

"I have no idea," Marve replied then pulled out his pocket watch. "But I do know we are on in ten," he said with a smile then turned and headed to the stage.

I slid open the box. Gently, I lifted a pair of new ballerina slippers from the box. The shocking red of the silk thereon was unlike anything I had ever seen. It was the red of a brand new rose, a heady, luxurious color.

At the bottom of the box was a folded note:

For Miss McKenna,

A small token of my gratitude and esteem.

Lord John Waldegrave.

I chuckled. A light in the darkness, here was an unexpected gift from John. Why hadn't Marve just told me it was from him? Perhaps he didn't want to ruin the surprise.

I slid off my boots and slipped on the red slippers. They were perfect. I tied the long red ribbons around my ankles.

"Oh, Elyse," Lizzie said in an excited gasp.

I turned to find her standing at the entrance of my section.

"They're so beautiful. Who are they from?" she asked.

"John." But I hadn't told him about what had happened to my old slippers, had I? I couldn't remember. Perhaps he just wanted to surprise me. I tied the other red silk ribbon into a neat bow then admired my feet.

"Such a fine gift. They're so lovely," she said with a smile. "So tonight is the night," she whispered in a low voice.

I nodded, feeling that terrible sense of dread once more.

Lizzie eyed me curiously, then her forehead furrowed. "Here, let me do your makeup," she said, lifting the blush brush.

I turned and faced her.

"Are you nervous?" Lizzie asked lightly, but there was an odd catch in her voice.

"I…I don't know what I am feeling today."

"And Doctor Murray? What has he to say on this matter?"

"He…he doesn't know."

At that, Lizzie stopped. "Elyse, are you very sure this is what you want?"

I looked down at the red slippers.

"Not the title, not the red slippers, is *he* the man you want? Do you love him?" Lizzie asked.

"I…it's what any of us dream of, isn't it? A fine title? A man of station? An estate and life of ease?"

"Maybe," Lizzie said. "Maybe, but if this is what you really want, why do you look so sad? Is it the elopement? We are actresses. An attachment with women of our station is always undesirable. Has he made you feel embarrassed?"

"No. He told me he was prepared for some gossip but that it would pass. No. It's not that, it's just…"

Lizzie looked at me. "Doctor Murray?"

I nodded. I felt my tears threaten.

"Don't cry. You'll ruin your makeup," Lizzie said with a soft smile.

I took a deep breath and steadied myself.

"Ah, my dear, what can we ladies do? I do not envy you this trouble, but if I can help you, you must tell me," Lizzie said.

"Thank you."

"Five minutes," Marve called.

Lizzie picked up the eye makeup brush. "Close your eyes, Persephone. It's almost time to be dragged to hell."

ONCE LIZZIE AND I WERE done, I hurried backstage where the others waited. Upon seeing me, Marve signaled to Skippy and a flutter of chimes sounded indicating that the show was about to begin.

I slipped off my coat, pulled my red slipper-covered feet from inside my boots, which I'd worn to protect the slippers from the snow, then straightened my costume.

"In a sunny meadow outside Athens, the Goddess Persephone brings forth spring's delights," Hannah, speaking as the chorus, announced. With a tinkle of chimes, the curtain opened.

I closed my eyes and tried to shut all my worries away. I was Persephone, the Goddess of spring. It was a sunny morning, and I was out picking flowers for my mother. Taking a deep breath, I took my first step in the red slippers. The shoes molded to my feet, the soft silk covering the stiff bones of the slipper keeping the foot in shape. I spun onto the stage, bending with graceful shapes, trying to echo the beauty of flowers growing in the meadow.

Dancing in the pantomimes was one of my favorite things to do on stage. Save the chorus, it was up to the actors to make the scenes work since there was little to no dialogue. All expression came from the face and movements of the actors. Bending gracefully, I pretended to pick flowers as Josiah played a light tune on a harp. I bent and danced, twirling on my new slippers which held my feet perfectly. How had John even known my size?

The movement of the scene was such that I hardly had a moment to pause. Only when the faux wind started to blow after I'd followed a random line of narcissus blossoms, leading me to the section of the stage where Hobbs as Hades waited for me, did I have a chance to scan the audience.

I looked quickly and in earnest for John but did not spy his familiar green jacket. The audience was mostly full, the rough benches lined with people, but it was not overflowing. It was not nearly as cold as it had been on prior days. I glanced out over the ice. Many more tents were gone.

The harp chimed a menacing tone, and I turned to see Hades, dressed in the mask of a plague doctor, emerge from his underground lair. He had come for me.

Slipping back into character, I was, once more, lost to Persephone.

Hades and I then raced about the stage, a commedia in truth, until I was taken to hell where I moped unhappily while the world above me froze. Only when my mother Demeter, as played by Agnes, came for me did I shine once more. Add in a scene with the juggling of pomegranates, a slapstick battle between Hades and Demeter, and the commedia was over.

There was only a fifteen-minute intermission until the showing of *Glass Slipper Girl*. I rushed to our backstage to slip into the costume of the faerie godmother. By the time I had finally changed, it was nearly time for the second performance to begin. When I returned to the backstage area, Lizzie had taken up my spot by the gap in the wooden slat and was looking out.

"Lizzie," I whispered. "Do you see John anywhere?"

She held up a finger then looked in earnest. "No," she whispered back to me, "but look just outside the tent." She leaned back so I could see.

Standing just outside was Marve and the Frost Fair marshall. The marshall was motioning to the stage while Marve listened, rocking back and forth on his feet.

"A large section of the ice below London Bridge cracked open.

I overheard some people talking in line when I stopped for a bun this morning," Lizzie whispered.

"Looks like we're being closed down," I said then leaned back.

Lizzie sighed. It was then that I noticed she was still wearing her snowflake pendant. It shimmered in the morning sunlight. A prism of rainbows cast all around the stage near us. I lifted my hand, letting the light refract on my palm.

Lizzie smiled. "You've caught a rainbow. And what about your mirror? Do you have it with you?"

"In my coat pocket."

"I didn't see your Frost Fair Prince this morning. He usually attends the shows."

I nodded.

Where had John gone? Was he planning to come back after the show? We needed to talk about what had happened with Kai and the plan for the evening. I still had no notion of when and where to meet him. Did he presume I would just get dolled up as a bride and sit and wait for him at the theatre? No. That was not his way. It was wrong of me to think so ill of him. But once more I remembered the man at the chocolate stand with the girl with the red bonnet. I was so certain it had been John.

"Elyse?" Lizzie said then, and I could tell by the sound of her voice it was not the first time she'd called my name.

I looked at my outstretched hand which still held the blob of rainbow-colored hues.

Lizzie slipped the pendant back inside her gown. The rainbows disappeared.

Marve was standing there. I realized then that I had missed the first part of the conversation.

"…so tonight will be the last performance. They're moving everyone off after ten. They expect the ice to start flowing in earnest by midday tomorrow if the warm weather persists."

The other actors moaned softly in protest.

A terrible thought gripped my heart. If the ice began to flow and Kai was still aboard Captain Behra's ship, then what? Would he leave with her? I bit my lip so hard it hurt.

"…nevertheless, the show must go on, but the Frost Fair is done after tonight's performance," Marve said.

At that, the company got busy preparing for our final performance of *Glass Slipper Girl*. I took the spot by the gap in the slat as the play began. Lizzie took center stage and prepared to be mistreated by Agnes, who now played the role of the wicked stepmother in Marion's absence.

I watched the commotion outside the Ice House Theatre. Wagons moved to and fro on the ice as everyone began to leave. The crowd, I noted, had thinned out for the second performance.

In no time, the poor cinder girl's wicked family had reduced her to tears and despair just hours before the ball was set to begin. Picking up my wand and readying myself in my red slippers, I once more took to the stage to give my faerie goddaughter a healthy dose of friendly faerie advice and a new pair of shoes. Before I knew it, the performance was done. I hurried backstage to change, leaving my Titania costume in Hannah's section before I headed back out onto the ice.

"Elyse," Skippy said, running up to me as I exited the tent. "A message."

I took the paper from him.

"Miss McKenna, may I request a few moments of your time? With my sincere thanks, Lord John Waldegrave."

"Where is he?" I asked Skippy, my brows furrowing. Was John trying to be funny?

"The gentleman? He's still inside," he said, motioning to the theatre.

Nodding, I put the note in my pocket and headed back into the theatre. When I arrived, the theatre was empty save Josiah clearing the last of the props from the stage. Tonight's performance would certainly be bare. Aside from Josiah, a gentleman stood in the middle of the theatre, his hands behind his back in the most proper of stances, as he watched Josiah work. He wore a fine top hat and a black coat cut from expensive-looking material. He had a fine cut and dark, curly hair, but he was not John.

"See you later, Elyse," Josiah called from the stage as he pushed one of the props, a snowy tree from the Forest of Arden, backstage.

At that, the gentleman turned.

Surprising me, the man smiled then removed his top hat. He bowed nicely then looked up at me. After a moment, he chuckled.

"Miss McKenna, I do believe you don't recognize me," he said.

"I'm…I'm sorry. I was looking for someone. My apologies. Do I…do I know you?"

He nodded and moved toward me. "Yes, indeed. Perhaps you'd recognize me better if I had a cloud of onion soup perfume hanging around me."

I gasped, realizing then that the gentleman was, in fact, the man who'd fallen into the ice. It was an exciting discovery, but where was John?

"Oh my goodness," I said. "It is so good to see you about, sir. I had inquired yesterday at the Hawkings' workshop but you were not in. I was relieved to hear you'd recovered yourself."

"Indeed, I have. And just in time, from what I have learned. Let me properly introduce myself, Miss McKenna. I am Lord John Waldegrave."

I felt my knees go soft. "Sorry?"

"Miss McKenna?" the man said, taking a step toward me. "Are you…are you all right?"

"What…what did you say your name is?"

"John Waldegrave," he said then moved forward to take my arm. "You look very pale. Please sit," he said. Leading me gently by the arm, he sat me down on a bench.

"That's not possible. Lord Waldegrave…I…"

Not understanding my confusion, the gentleman began. "Ah, yes.

Well, the long story short of it was that I was on commission in France as a member of the twelfth light Dragoons, but our mission ended so I've returned to England. I was in London to look after my family's investments in a mercantile venture which is, apparently, how I understood the fabric of your slipper so well. Unfortunately, someone used my absence to make use of my name and bank account. Apparently, some rogue has been running up debts in my name. I was here at the Frost Fair making inquiries into the matter. The last things I recall are stopping here to see your show. Thereafter, I went to the City of Moscow for a drink, where some rowdy chaps rewarded my service to the crown with more Scotch than was fitting. The next thing I knew, I woke up in a barrel of onion soup with your pretty face looking at me in a fit of concern. As near as we can tell, my counterfeit saw fit to put me underwater when he discovered I'd returned from abroad and was inquiring behind him. The rogue wearing my name and title has racked up a fortune in gambling debts and other expenses, and from what the constables have been able to tell, a few broken hearts have been left in his wake. My mother had a pretty young lass turn up at her doorstep looking for her husband, Lord Waldegrave, only to find out the truth. Poor girl. I say, Miss McKenna, are you quite all right?"

"Yes. Yes, I'm fine. The story is…shocking, that is all. And have they caught the rogue?"

"I am afraid not. But we'll have him in no time. The young lady helped us track him back to a minister who has been blessing his false unions for a few coins. Apparently, he's scheduled to bring another maid by tonight."

"But...why? Why wed the girl then abandon her? Was she well-off?"

The gentleman stiffened. "Alas, Miss McKenna, it seems some men's devices are more devious than that. The most devilish of men will stoop to the lowest levels to win the hearts of otherwise virtuous and unobtainable ladies. And to think that such deeds were done in my name. I...I cannot bear the thought. But let's turn to something less odious. How do you find your slippers? I say, you turned very prettily in them."

I looked up at him. Taking a deep breath, I pulled on the face of a woman who had no cares in the world. I did not want him to see the terror that was about to break through the surface. I pressed my emotions down and felt nothing, only shaped myself as the mask of a calm theatre actress who has just been paid a very nice compliment from a proper gentleman.

"I thank you, sir. They are very beautiful and fit so perfectly. How did you ever guess my size?"

He smiled, then from his pocket he pulled one of the pink slippers my grandmother had given me. "You forgot your slipper, Cinderella."

I gasped.

"I thought it was very...fortuitous," he said, handing the slipper back to me.

I reached out and took it then looked up at him. Lord John Waldegrave—the real Lord John Waldegrave—smiled nicely at me. He was everything a gentleman should be. Well-dressed, eloquently spoken, and very proper. But there was a hopeful look in his countenance that was more than I could bear.

I rose.

"Miss McKenna," he said, rising along with me.

"I…I'm very sorry, Lord Waldegrave, but I'm afraid you're right. I am not feeling well. I should very much like to talk over this matter with you at another time. I think I have some infor—I have something I must see to first, and I am not quite myself at the moment. Please forgive me. May I send you a note and call later?"

He nodded. Taking a card from his pocket, he handed it to me. "Please. Whenever you're feeling up to it. I owe my life to you and Doctor Murray. My family, as well, is keen to meet you both. My mother is such a fan of the theatre. Really, the Waldegraves are all quite indebted to you."

My stomach churned, and I almost vomited. Taking a deep breath, I said, "I do so appreciate the slippers. They are…they are truly beautiful. Thank you so very much. Now, I must—if you will please excuse me, I must—I—I'll be in touch very soon," I said, then curtseyed. I turned and headed away from the theatre in the direction of Captain Behra's ship.

24
ON NOT LETTING IT GO

AS I APPROACHED THE SHIP, I saw that the sailors were moving busily. It looked like they were preparing for the inevitable departure. They eyed me skeptically as I neared but didn't say a word. One man looked me over then went inside the captain's quarters. Not waiting for permission, I walked up the plank and headed toward the door to the captain's cabin. The sailors stopped to watch.

I had just reached the door when one of the men stepped out, blocking my way. I peered through the open door of the captain's cabin. There, I saw Kai sitting on the floor, his back resting against the bed, his chin on his chest. His hair was a tousled mess that hung over his face.

"Kai," I yelled. "Kai!"

At the sound of my voice, Kai looked up. His eyes met mine, but he didn't seem to recognize me.

The sailor closed the door behind him. "The captain said you should go away."

"I will not," I said sharply then tried to push the man aside. "Kai? Kai! Kai, do you hear me? Kai?" I yelled.

The large man grabbed me by the waist and set me down in front of him once more.

"The captain said that you should leave, and if you do not, I should remove you."

"Tell your captain to come out here and move me herself, if she is woman enough," I shouted toward the door, hoping to provoke Captain Behra's ire. "Kai! Kai, come out here right now! Kai, I need you. Kai, get up and get out here!"

The sailor laughed. "Silly little ballerina," he said then picked me up and threw me over his shoulder. "You don't know who you are dealing with."

"Kai! Kai! Help me," I yelled, hoping the panic in my voice would rouse him.

The sailors stood watching, mixed expressions of empathy and annoyance on their faces. Amongst them, I spotted Robin. My eyes met his, and through the windows of our souls, I pleaded with him.

"Put her down," Robin called to the sailor.

The sailor laughed and walked down the plank.

"Kai! Kai, do you hear me?" I yelled, looking back at the cabin.

There was no movement from inside.

I looked back toward where Robin was standing, but the boy was gone.

"I'm going to bring the Bow Street Runners," I told the sailor. "I'll have you all arrested for abduction. Doctor Murray is a well-respected physician in this city. They won't let you hold him hostage like this."

"The only thing he is hostage to is what's between the captain's thighs. A beautiful prison at that, and he doesn't seem to mind," the sailor said with a laugh.

I scanned the crowd of men, expecting to see them laughing, but instead, I found worried expressions on their faces.

"Liar," I said. "Put me down right now."

When we reached the end of the plank, the sailor deposited me back onto the ice. "The river will flow by morning. Your doctor is with us now. Don't come back, ballerina."

Furious, I reached down and grabbed a handful of snow. Clenching it into a ball, I hurled it at the man. "You won't get away with this," I told him.

He laughed, brushing the snow off his shoulder.

Frowning, I turned and stormed away. I could go to the Bow Street Runners. Certainly, they would come to investigate, but they might also be easily convinced that Kai wanted to be there. No. There was still one card left to play, and with any luck, it was the best card in the deck.

A king always trumps a queen.

25
FROZEN HEARTS

I WOVE MY WAY DOWN Freezeland Lane. Carts and wagons waited as tents were struck down. No more oil cakes nor ice cream was to be had. Even The Frozen Mushroom had closed up shop. When the bawds moved out, it was surely time to go.

I headed in the direction of the ice castle and the other ship frozen into the Thames. If I was going to find the baron, certainly that would be my best bet. Out of options, I could only hope he would be willing to contend with his quarreling wife on my behalf.

I was just passing the City of Moscow when someone called my name.

"Elyse? Is that you? Elyse?" I stopped and looked back. To my shock, John—and not the real John, of course, but the rake—stood there, a smile on his face. "My dear, I've been looking everywhere for you."

Caught up in a torrent of fury, I turned on my heel, crossed the ice, and then promptly smacked John across the face. I ripped off my glove then tore the ring from my finger and threw it in his face.

John clutched his face where I struck him. "Elyse?"

"Don't even speak my name, you liar," I spat angrily.

"What are you talking about? Whatever's the matter? I was looking for you. I wanted to talk to you about tonig—"

"Shut your lying mouth," I replied.

"Elyse? What happen—"

"What happened? What happened? This morning I met the real Lord John Waldegrave. In fact, Doctor Murray and I saved Lord Waldegrave's life after a rogue, a pretender, tried to murder him. That same pretender has been roaming around London racking up debts and breaking hearts. How could you? How could you do that to me?"

"But how—what did you—did you tell him about me?" he stammered. His face had gone completely pale.

"And what, exactly, would I tell him? That I am just as much of a fool as every other girl you've been lying to? That I believed you actually loved me? That I trusted you? Why me? Why in the world would you play such a game with me? Who am I to you? I'm no one. I never did anything to you, to anyone. Was all this just to...merely because you wanted to bed me? Was that all? Why not just spend the coin and ride a whore? Why bother me?"

"Because someone like you would never look at a man like me without a fancy title. You, who denies the likes of Lord Byron, would never accept a low-born gardener's son. I'm nothing. No one. If you'll deny Byron, why would you love me?"

"Byron? What does Byron have to do with it?"

"I saw him at the theatre when he propositioned you. You would not have him. And if you would not have him, why would you ever take a man like me?" John said. The look on his face was a mix of shame and anger. By all appearances, he was a man shattered, but his excuses hurt almost as much as his lies. How could he think so low of me?

"I didn't accept Byron because he is a bawd and because I do not love him. I am an actress, John—or whatever your name is—I'm not some fine lady. I can love an honest man no matter his station, high or low, but not a rogue or a liar."

He laughed ruefully. "You won't even accept your doctor friend. Do you really expect me to believe you'd let someone like me bed you? Now, who is lying?"

"Don't turn this on me. My heart is open to an honest man. If you really cared for me, you never would have tricked me. At what point were you planning to tell me who you really are? Once you had my maidenhead? Is that all this is about to you? A game to win a place in my bed for the night? No doubt you would have rid of me once you'd bedded me as you did with that other girl."

John paled even further, revealing I had come close to the truth. "Wh—what other girl?"

"Perhaps the girl you were with at the chocolate stand? The girl with the red bonnet? I imagine she must be the ruined girl who appeared to the Waldegraves in search of her husband."

John laughed. "Fine, Elyse. Have it your way. But you fell for the title, didn't you? How else could I ever get your attention? I wanted you, Elyse. I did what I had to in order make you mine. Judge yourself for being so shallow."

"The title never mattered to me. It was your words, your lies, that I loved."

"That's rich."

I shook my head, choking down my tears. "If you had treated me honestly, everything would have been different. But it was never about that. I was only a prize for you."

"A prize? Oh yes, you're Frostiana, aren't you, queen of the frozen Thames? Indeed, there was quite a wager as to whether or not I would win your frozen heart and see if you were just as cold between your legs."

"Liar. You first saw me at Struthers Theatre at Christmastime. This has nothing to do with the Frost Fair. Why lie now? You know very well that I came to love you. I believed your lies, and I loved you," I said. The tears I had fought so hard finally choked me.

He blew air between his lips in an attitude of dismissal, but the tremble of his chin told another story.

"And you loved me too. Despite the lie," I added. "In fact, you were trapped by the lie, weren't you? You fell in love with me, but didn't know how to tell me the truth."

At that, he paused. I was right. He had lied to win me in the first place, and that lie had been motivated out of carnal desire. Perhaps he'd only hoped to win me for the night, but I could see from the expression on his face that it had gone beyond that.

"Elyse," he said softly, a guilty expression on his face.

"Go away. Leave the ice. Even if you did love me, you still played with that other woman. Aside from what happened between us, there is the matter of what you did to the real Lord Waldegrave. Go. Go back to wherever you came from, or I'll call the Bow Street Runners right now and turn you in."

"You wouldn't do that."

"I would. Your lies, including your promise to help Doctor Murray, have left my friend in danger. I trusted you blindly, and my heart will pay for that. But through me, you struck at someone I care about, and I cannot forgive you that. Leave. Now."

"You won't turn me in, will you? They'll send me to the Tower if they find me."

"Leave. Now."

"Elyse—"

"Never speak my name again. Now go."

At that, the man I knew as John, turned. He stopped for a moment, looking down at the engagement ring which had fallen to the ice, then turned and walked away.

I looked down at the glittering piece of jewelry. It lay there, an innocent victim in our feud. After a moment's hesitation, I scooped it up. It was very pretty, shimmering in the afternoon sun. I sighed. At least I could give it to the real Lord Waldegrave so he could recoup some of his lost fortunes. After all, it was not fair that he—the innocent person in all this mess—be harmed anymore. As much as I never wanted to see the ring again, I slipped it into my pocket then turned once more in the direction of the baron's ship, my heart completely shattered.

26
THE BARON

MY HANDS TREMBLED AS I neared the ship. A single gentleman lingered on board. He smoked a pipe and watched as I approached. When I drew close, the man rose and went to the captain's cabin. A moment later, the baron appeared on the deck. He held the rail tightly, a bit too tightly, as he watched me approach.

"Miss McKenna?" he called.

"You wife has taken my friend prisoner. I need your help to get him back."

"My…my wife?"

"Captain Behra. I know about the two of you. Somehow Kai and I have fallen in the middle of whatever marital discord you are experiencing, but I don't care anything about it. I don't care that she is angry at you. I don't care who hurt whom first. I don't care about anything but Kai. And right now, you are the only one who can help me."

The baron grabbed a rope and slid down to the ice, a flourish of fine velvet fabric twirling around him.

The baron's man tossed him down his walking stick.

He straightened his clothes then turned and joined me, the picture of a gentlemanly figure.

"Let's walk," he said, taking my arm. "You...you are right. By chance, Captain Behra and I both found ourselves in port when the Thames froze, trapping us and our problems here. The captain became aware that I admired your performance so sought to punish you by corrupting your friend. I must apologize that you've been pulled into this petty disagreement between my wife and me. She struck at you unfairly, and I am ashamed to say I sought to hurt her further when she turned her affections toward your friend. But this has gone too far. Soon the river will thaw. This must come to an end."

"They told me she's going to take Kai with her. I don't understand. Kai would never leave me like this."

"He is under her influence and unable to act of his own accord."

"Then you must help me recover him before it's too late. You must take him from the ship."

"I cannot."

"Then you have to talk to her, reason with her, lie to her. I don't care what you need to do, but you need to do it."

The baron smiled. "You misunderstood my meaning. I cannot get your friend off the ship, but you can."

"Me? How can I possibly do that? Her henchman carried me off the ship by force today."

"I have a plan."

"A plan?"

"Your troupe…do you have access to the men's costumes? Perhaps the cinder girl's father's attire?"

"Men's costumes? Why?"

The baron smiled. "Because at dusk, we shall get Doctor Murray off my wife's ship."

27
HONEST IAGO

BY THE TIME THE BARON and I finalized the plan, it was nearly dusk. I headed back to the Ice House Theatre where the others were preparing for the final performance of *A Midwinter Night's Dream*.

"Elyse?" Marve said when he saw me approached the tent. "We weren't expecting you. Hannah is inside preparing for the part of Titania. Should I tell her to—"

"No. But I need your wagon, and I need one of Robert's costumes."

"My wagon and—what? Elyse, what's going on?"

Hearing my voice, Lizzie came out of the tent, half prepared for her role as Hermia.

"Elyse? What are you doing here?" The expression on her face was a storm of questions. If I was at the Ice House then I wasn't busy eloping.

By way of explanation, I shook my head then said, "Change of plans, I'm afraid."

"Change of plans? What happened?" Lizzie asked.

"I'll tell you tomorrow. Right now, I need your help. Can I have the wagon? I'll be back with it before the show ends," I said, turning to Marve.

"Of course. Elyse, are you in trouble?" Marve asked, his forehead furrowing.

"I just need the wagon…and the costume."

"Certainly," Marve said.

Taking Lizzie by the arm, I said, "Will you help me?"

She nodded.

With a smile of appreciation to Marve, Lizzie and I turned and headed into the dressing tent.

"Robert?" I called.

He stepped out from behind his dressing curtain. He was already ready for the night's performance. "Elyse? What is it?"

"I need your matinee costume," I said as we joined him in his section. "And your beard," I added, pointing to the hairpiece that sat waiting alongside his stage makeup.

"My beard? Why?" Robert asked.

"I am Viola turned Cesario tonight," I said, referring to Master Shakespeare's ill-fated heroine who disguised herself as a man to survive in a foreign country in his play *Twelfth Night*.

Clearly concerned, Robert frowned but said nothing more. "Very well. Let's make with the masculine trappings then. Sit," he added, motioning for me to take a seat.

A few moments later, Robert got to work applying the sticky resin that would hold the beard onto my face.

"Elyse, what happened?" Lizzie asked as Robert got the costume ready.

"John was a liar, no more, no less," I said. My heart ached, and yet I chided myself. My instincts had been screaming at me from the start that he was not to be trusted, but still, I wanted to believe him. Why? Was he right? Was I so desperate for a title? How had I been so stupidly duped? I felt ridiculous. But John was wrong about one thing, it was not the title I'd wanted. I'd wanted a faerie tale. The love affair had all the usual trappings: poor orphaned girl meets a rich handsome gentleman, rich handsome gentleman sweeps her off her feet, rich handsome gentleman proposes. And then, the happily ever after, right? But nothing really works like that. Not even the real faerie tales. After all, Snow White had to die to find a man who really loved her. I should have known better. I should have trusted the voice inside me that knew John was false. And worse, I should not have left Kai's fate in the hands of a man I'd loved quickly and foolishly.

Lizzie sighed. "So many times we are played the fool. When will we ever learn we shouldn't fall in love with a man we just met?"

"Such men ruin the name of honest gentlemen. Speaking of which, honest Iago," Richard said, lifting the beard.

I nodded.

Robert worked quickly applying it to my face. After a few moments, he stood back then nodded. "You make a very ugly man, Miss McKenna."

In spite of myself, I laughed. Remembering the mirror in my pocket, I pulled it out and looked at my reflection. The beard looked a bit like I'd glued a beaver to my face. He was right, I was a very ugly man. But in the dim twilight, it would do its job.

"Let me brush your hair back," Lizzie said. She pulled my hair back into a tight coif like gentlemen sometimes wore.

Robert handed me the costume then turned to go, but he paused first and said, "Elyse, I don't know what manner of trouble you're in, but please be careful."

"Thank you," I said with a soft smile.

He nodded then left.

"He's right, you know. And just where are you going with this manly costume and Marve's wagon?" Lizzie asked.

My heart slammed hard in my chest. I didn't have time to be afraid. I fought off the fear that wanted to overwhelm me. There was nothing I wouldn't do for Kai.

"I'm going to save my friend."

"Your friend?"

"Doctor Murray."

"Ah, so you're going to save the man you really love," Lizzie said.

I froze in place at her words then looked into the little hand mirror, remembering the fleeting vision I'd seen there the night before. The man I really loved? Was she right? I bit my bottom lip then nodded.

"Yes," I whispered, the word seeming like an admission that had come from deep within my heart. "Yes."

28
WHAT ELYSE SAID

DRESSED AS THE CINDER GIRL'S father, my fake beard itching, I drove the wagon toward The Frozen Mermaid. There, one of the baron's men stood outside waiting. When I first arrived, the man did not recognize me. Only when I signaled to him did he nod in affirmation then went inside. I waited a few moments more. Then the baron and ten of his gentlemen emerged. Upon seeing me, the baron smirked. He tipped the brim of his hat toward me then turned and headed toward Captain Behra's ship.

Taking my cue, I clicked to Marve's mule, then directed the wagon across the ice. As I drove near the captain's ship, a few of the sailors gave me a hard look. It was the moment of truth. I drove, looking as though I was intent on a destination somewhere further down the ice, and tried to hold my body in a manly posture. Not finding me of interest, the men looked away. I rode into the dark then slowed the wagon.

"Tia!" I heard the baron yell. I looked back. He and his men stood at the end of the plank. "Tia, come out here." His voice sounded far sterner than I had ever heard it in the past.

The sailors on Captain Behra's ship moved down the plank, their weapons drawn.

I kept my face shadowed but watched as a very annoyed looking Captain Behra finally appeared on deck.

"Ill met by moonlight, proud Tia," the baron called.

"What, jealous baron? Get hence. You know I've forsworn your company."

"Perhaps, but would you hear my apology?" the baron called in reply.

That was my cue. Snapping the reigns, I moved the mule cart in a wide arch that circled back to the far side of the Captain's ship. I spared just one last glance back.

Captain Behra smirked. Gripping her sword, she pushed past her men as she made her way down the plank.

I inhaled deeply and drove the cart to the back of the captain's ship.

I listened as the baron and the captain exchanging barbs.

And I waited.

The baron would keep his promise.

Everything would go as planned.

He owed it to me.

He would keep his promise.

A few moments later, there was a cheer from the other side of the ship. I waited.

One of the torches on my side of the ship suddenly went dark. A rope ladder dropped over the rail.

I looked up to see the smiling face of the boy, Robin, looking down at me. He winked at me then disappeared. I waited a few more moments, listening as the sound of voices faded into the night. It had worked. The captain and her men had joined with the baron's and were moving away from the ship.

Hands shaking, I tied off the reins then crawled into the back of the wagon. Taking hold of the rope ladder, I gave it a tug. It seemed to be securely attached. I bit my lip, steeled my nerve, and climbed up. When I reached the rail, I peered on board. There was no one on deck. At the end of the plank, one of the captain's men stood sentinel.

Moving quietly, I slipped onto the ship. Keeping low, I sneaked toward the door of the captain's cabin. I carefully lifted the latch and snuck inside. My heart pounded in my chest. The room within was very dim. It took my eyes a moment to adjust to the light. Only a few candles lit the space. The heavy scents of alcohol and opium lingered in the air. Plates with pomegranates and other fruits sat half-eaten. Moving quickly, I rushed toward the captain's bed where Kai lay half unconscious.

"Kai," I whispered, rolling him over.

His shirt was undone. He looked like he'd been sweating, and his skin was very pale. The scents of smoke and drink wafted off of him.

"Kai," I said, shaking his shoulder.

He frowned at that. "Don't touch me. I told you I do not want you. Stop touching me."

My stomach churned hard. Tears pricked the corners of my eyes. "For the love of all things holy, Kai. Please, wake up."

This time, he opened his eyes. When he looked at me, he frowned. "Captain, the fungi you gave me is having the strangest effect on me. I see Elyse in the face of your sailor. You know, I really must be going soon. She'll be worried," he said then closed his eyes once more, chuckling stupidly.

His words and the terrible condition he was in evoked such a rage in me that I wanted to choke the captain to death.

"Kai, it's me. I'm disguised. You need to come with me. Kai, wake up," I said, shaking him again.

Kai's eyes opened momentarily. He studied my face. "Elyse?"

"It's me. Now, you need to get up before the captain returns. We need to go. Now."

"I feel sick. Elyse, tell Gram to come get me," he said then closed his eyes once more.

At that, I grabbed him by the arms and tried to pull him from the bed. He was limp and heavy. I slid his legs to the side of the bed then tried to lift him. It was no use. I tugged hard, trying to lift him, but we both ended up on the floor. I set my head on his chest.

"Kai. Kai, please. I cannot do this alone," I whispered. "You are not yourself. You need to leave with me now, or we will never see one another again. We will lose one another forever." Reaching up, I pulled off my beard and stuck it into my pocket. Everything was in ruins. If I couldn't get Kai to leave with me, then I would have to stay and face the captain.

"It's okay," I said then, brushing a lock of his hair away from his forehead. "It's okay. I'll stay with you. I won't leave you here. If you can't leave, then neither will I," I said. "Kai, do you hear me?"

"Elyse?" he whispered softly. "My stomach feels strange."

I set my head on his shoulder. Tears rolled down my cheeks, wetting his shirt. Taking a deep breath, I looked up. I wiped my tears then reached up and touched his cheek. "Kai, I love you," I whispered. "I love you with all of my heart and all my soul. I've been a very foolish girl. The idea of losing you…I cannot live without you. Kai, I love you," I said. Leaning in, I placed a soft kiss on his lips.

At first, there was no reaction. His lips were warm and soft, but he didn't return my kiss.

I kissed him harder then, putting my hands on his cheeks, pressing his body closer to mine.

This time, however, he pulled back.

"No," he said, a sharp, angry tone in his voice. "No. You have no right. Get away from me. My heart belongs to only one woman."

My stomach clenched into a hard ball.

I was too late.

"I'm sorry," I whispered then pulled back.

At the sound of my voice, he looked up at me once more. This time, however, his eyes were clear. His brow furrowed deeply as though he was just coming to himself.

"Elyse?" he whispered.

He looked around, a confused expression on his face. "The captain? Where did that whore go? She was just here. She tried to—Elyse?"

"Yes. Yes, I know. And we need to go. Now. Before she returns. Can you stand up?" I asked. Rising to my feet, I reached down for him.

"I'll bloody well try."

Steadying myself, I helped Kai stand. Once he was firmly on his feet, I led him to the door. Moving quietly, I unlatched the door and peered outside. The captain's man was no longer at the end of the platform. I didn't see him anywhere on the ship.

Wrapping my arm around Kai's waist, I nodded to him. "Come with me. Quiet."

Wordlessly, Kai followed me to the rail of the ship. I could tell he was weak on his feet, but there was no helping it. I had the baron's word that he would keep the captain away, but he may not be able to manage for long. What would happen when the captain realized she had been fooled? We needed to hurry.

"There is a ladder here. You'll have to climb down. Can you make it?"

I whispered.

"Yes." I could tell from the sound of his voice that he was trying to sound confident, but his slumping body told a different tale.

"I'll go first and try to steady you," I said. Making sure Kai had hold of the rail, I swung over the side of the ship and started down the rope, moving quickly to the wagon below.

"Kai. Now you," I said.

Moving slowly, Kai crawled over the rail.

My heart slammed in my chest as I watched him struggle to hold on to the ropes. His foot slipped as he tried to feel for the rung.

I tugged on the rope ladder, guiding the rung under his foot.

"Doctor? Where are you going?" the captain's henchman yelled from the deck of the ship.

Kai moved with purpose then, trying to get down the ladder.

The sailor appeared at the side of the ship above us, glaring down. He stared at Kai, then me, his eyes narrowing. He pulled his sword from his belt and lifted it.

"Kai! Jump," I called.

Kai turned and leaped into the wagon. He grunted a little as he landed, but landed all the same.

A second later, the sailor dropped his sword on the rope ladder. It fell half in and half out of the wagon.

"Go," Kai called weakly.

I snatched up the reins and snapped them, clicking loudly to the mule who must have been dozing.

From the deck of the ship, an odd-sounding trumpet signaled loudly. Its warning sound echoed across the ice.

"Oh, Bottom. Move, please," I called to the mule, snapping the reins again. This time, the mule got some spring in his step, and he rushed quickly away. I moved the mule carefully across the ice at a quick clip. We were already a good distance from the ship when I heard shouting.

A sharp wind blew, and with it, a fog seemed to roll across the Thames, enveloping the space between the Frost Fair and the riverside in a thick mist. I clicked at the mule and drove the wagon off the ice toward the city. Only once we were off the ice did I look back at Kai. He sat slumped along the side of the wagon. He was not himself, but he was there. That was all that mattered. I needed to get him somewhere safe quickly.

I turned the cart in the direction of the Hawkings' workshop. He could rest there until he regained his composure. I drove down the bumpy cobblestone street, focusing so completely on my task that I didn't stop until the wagon pulled in front of the Hawkings' home.

I rapped loudly on the door then waited, staring pensively back out at the ice. My heart thundered in my chest for fear that the captain would chase me here to seek out her revenge. Perhaps Master Shakespeare had taught me to expect too much drama. This wasn't *Hamlet*, after all.

"Miss McKenna?" the footman said.

Master Hawking and Isabelle appeared in the foyer behind the servant.

"Miss McKenna?" Master Hawking said, coming to the door.

"It's Doctor Murray," I said, turning toward the cart. "He's unwell."

Without another word, Master Hawking, Isabelle, the servant, and I went to the wagon where Kai sat staring at the frozen river, his brow furrowed in anger.

"Kai," I said, setting my hand on his shoulder. He was startled by my touch but then softened when he looked at me. "Kai. Come inside. Master Hawking will see to you. You'll be safe here," I said, whispering the last.

He nodded grimly then slid off the back of the wagon. I slipped one of his arms over my shoulder while Master Hawking took the other. I noticed that he was walking with a limp.

"What happened?" Isabelle asked, her wide dark eyes taking in the situation.

"Bad people doing bad things," I answered.

Isabelle led us to the parlor just off the main foyer. She moved a stack of books from a chaise, and Master Hawking and I lowered Kai into the seat.

"Elyse, my ankle," he whispered, seemingly embarrassed. "Can you remove my boot?"

I nodded then unlaced his boot, slipping it off. It was already swelling.

I turned to Isabelle. "Can you bring some ice?"

She nodded then rushed out of the room.

"Kai, are you all right? Shall I call the Bow Street Runners?" Master

Hawking asked, a distressed look on his face.

Kai shook his head. "No. I'll be fine now."

"I am so very sorry to bring another problem to your door, Master Hawking. It seemed urgent to get Kai somewhere safe," I said.

Master Hawking placed his hands behind his back then nodded affirmatively. "From the smell of you, Kai, I'd almost think Elyse just pulled you out of an opium den."

Kai frowned. "There has been some subterfuge done to me, I am ashamed to say."

Master Hawking nodded as he rubbed his chin. "I think I have something that will help if that is the case. I'll be back in a moment," he said, leaving us alone.

I sat down on the chaise beside Kai then stared into my hands as I bit my bottom lip, trying to think of what to say. So much had happened. So much had gone awry. I shook my head and blinked back my tears.

"Elyse?" Kai finally whispered.

I took a deep breath then looked up at him.

"I love you too. With all my soul. My mind is cloudy. I don't quite understand what has happened, but I do remember some things. I...I, too, have been a very silly man. And, I admit, a jealous man. I don't know how to live without you. I can't. Don't...please don't leave me. Elyse, I love you," he whispered then reached out and wiped a tear off my cheek. "I can't live without you."

"I love you too." I leaned in and placed the gentlest of kisses on his lips. This time, I was met with the full force of the man I'd known my whole life. I'd spent each day at his side, a friend, a companion. But it had always been more. He had always been a part of me. Why didn't I see that it was more than friendship? It had always been the deepest of loves.

"Oh," a little voice squeaked from the door.

Reluctantly, I pulled back and looked to find Isabelle standing there.

A wave of emotions washed over her face: frustration, jealousy, understanding, and then acceptance. In one swift moment, it seemed that Miss Hawking had accepted that any hopes she'd had for her and Kai were not meant to be. She beamed a bright and honest smile toward us.

"Here is the ice," she said, holding a cloth. "I went outside for it. A man passed by, told me the Thames is breaking up below the bridge. They are evacuating the ice as quickly as possible," she said, seeming to look for any bit of conversation to change the subject. "It's like a parade passing out there."

"Oh no," I whispered, turning back to Kai. "I have Marve's wagon. My troupe."

Kai nodded, understanding at once. "Don't leave me long, and please be careful."

"Don't worry. Just stay here and rest. I'll be back as soon as I can."

Kai kissed my hand then nodded to me as I turned and rushed to the door. If I didn't hurry, the Ice House and all of her belongings would sink into the Thames.

I slipped into the wagon once more and grabbed the reins. Clicking at the mule, I turned the cart and headed quickly back to the ice.

29
SEEING STARS

MY HANDS SHOOK AS I drove the wagon back onto the river. Everything was in commotion as the Bow Street Runners had joined the Frost Fair officials in hurrying everyone off the ice. Rows of carts rushed both on and off the ice. I snapped the reins and pushed Bottom toward the Ice House. My eyes scanned the crowd for the baron and the captain. With the river cracking open, surely the captain had better things to do than worry about Kai and me.

Speeding quickly down the ice, I soon reached the Ice House. I pulled the wagon up to the tent.

Marve, Hobbs, and Amy were rushing from the back of the theatre to the tents, their arms loaded, when I arrived.

"Oh, Elyse. Thank god," Marve exclaimed when he saw me.

"I'm so sorry. I just heard. I came as quick as I could," I said. I eyed the others. They were all still dressed in costume. "Did they stop you mid-performance?"

Marve nodded. "Titania's bower scene. And we really had the crowd too. But come. Quickly. We must load everything that's left at once and get off the ice. They said the first few ships nearest the bridge have already started to drift, some of the vendors' tents went under the ice."

And then, as if on cue, we heard a loud crack in the ice in the distance. The frozen river under our feet seemed to lurch.

The four of us exchanged glances. They headed toward the wagon while I rushed into the tent.

"The wagon is here. Everyone. Quickly," I called.

Upon hearing my voice, Lizzie and Robert ran toward the front of the tent.

"Elyse," Lizzie said, dropping the bundle of costumes she was holding. She pulled me into an embrace. "Are you all right? Did everything go as planned?"

"Yes, yes. Thank you, both. Kai is safe. Now, we must hurry."

They nodded.

Lizzie squeezed my arms, bent to pick up her bundle, then rushed toward the wagon. I headed into the back, passing Hannah and Skippy as they rushed out with a trunk. After them, James and Josiah toted mirrors toward the wagon.

"What can I do?" I asked.

"In the very back, the last of Marion's old wardrobe," Josiah said.

Taking a lantern, I headed toward the back of the tent.

There, I found the last trunk of clothes. It was open. The elaborate costumes Marion had worn lay spilled in the straw. I righted the chest then stuffed the costumes back inside.

I shivered as a hard wind kicked open the back flap of the tent. The chilled air swirled around me. For a brief moment, I felt the dark presence of someone standing behind me.

And then, I felt a terrible searing pain on my skull.

After that, there was only the stars.

30
THE CLOSING CURTAIN

I WOKE, MY HEAD ACHING. I felt terribly dizzy.

There was an odd sound like someone was chopping wood. Sprays of cold water splashed onto my face. I winced.

"You're to blame. You. Not me. This is your fault," a muddled voice growled at me.

I opened my eyes a crack to see a figure driving a pick-axe into the frozen river. We were on a dark section of the frozen river. I looked up and saw London Bridge near us.

Water splashed onto my face again.

"You couldn't just let him go, could you? Don't lie and tell me you didn't want him. I know you did. All along, it was him you wanted."

I squinted, trying to see, but my head ached miserably. The bitter taste of salt and metal tinged my mouth. Blood? I tried to make out the figure standing above me, but my eyes fluttered closed.

There was a sharp tug on my foot then a curse as the large man's boot I was wearing came off.

"Red slippers," the figure growled, then grabbed me by the ankle and pulled me across the ice. I felt the chill on the back of my neck, and something inside me screamed that I should wake up.

When I opened my eyes, I was looking up at the moon.

I tried to jerk my leg away from the rough hand that held it.

The figure stopped.

I shuddered with cold, and fear, and pain.

"Awake? No matter. It's done now."

The figure bent down and grabbed me roughly by the arm.

John.

"J—J—John?" I said through chattering teeth.

"Jacob, actually," he said. "Not that it would have mattered to you. You're such a whore. You ran from me right to him, didn't you? You were the liar all along, Elyse. Not me. You did this. You forced this on me. You. This is your fault," he said then tugged my arm. "You deserve this."

"What? No," I whispered.

"And now, after all your pretty talk, you'll give me up. You led me on. You spurned me. And now, no doubt, you'll turn me over to the law. Oh no. I won't die just because you couldn't love me as I was. It was your fault

I lied. I won't go to the Tower for your pretty face."

He tugged hard. The cold river water hit me with such terrible force that it knocked the wind out of me. Yet at the same time, something very mean in me took over. I knew that if I didn't act, and act now, I would die.

I reached out and felt for something, anything, to hold on to. There was nothing but water.

I opened my eyes. I was under the waves. Everything was black.

The movement of the Thames below the ice tugged at me, pulled me down.

I fought it. I gazed up through the water. I saw John's distorted image, the moon at his back, as he stood over the crack in the ice watching me die.

Kicking hard, I reached out and grabbed at the edge of the ice. It was sharp as glass. I pulled, trying to lift myself out of the water, but the Thames would not have it. I felt the dark water drag at me as my lungs burned.

I pulled myself toward the surface, but the ice I held onto gave way, coming off in a frozen chunk. I began slipping underwater.

I kicked hard, feeling the other boot give way. I kicked my legs like my life depended on it, and grabbed for the edge once more. But missed. My head hit the ice hard and I saw stars.

My lungs burned.

And it grew dark.

And cold.

And still.

If we shadows have offended...

If we shadows have offended.,.

If we shadows have offended...

31
THE CURTAIN CALL

AS THE LAST BREATH OF air left me, I opened my eyes once more.

John stood above me, watching me drown.

But a moment later, another figure appeared behind him. They lifted something large and dropped it on John's head. He crumpled.

Hands plunged into the water.

I kicked hard, reaching upward.

My hands connected with another's. Someone took me by the hands and pulled me from the river. I coughed hard, retching river water. The unseen person knelt behind me, patting my back as I wheezed, gasping for air.

"Elyse, breathe. Breathe! Cough out the water."

In the distance, I heard the whistle of one of the Bow Street Runners.

I coughed, water clearing from my lungs. It burned as it expelled from my nose and mouth. It hurt, but I was alive.

I opened my eyes just a crack and saw people carrying torches rushing toward me. In the crowd was one of the uniformed lawmen.

"What's happened here? Is she alive?" the Bow Street Runner asked in an authoritative voice.

"Barely. This man tried to drown her. I plucked her out in time," a feminine voice replied.

"What happened to him?"

"I cracked him on the head with guard of this sword. He's out," the person replied matter-of-factly.

"Arrest him. You there, lift the girl. She needs to be taken somewhere warm. Let's get her off the ice."

Strong hands lifted me. My head bobbed drowsily then leaned against a barrel-chested gentleman I didn't know.

"Your name, Madame?"

I opened my mouth to speak, but could only cough.

"My name is Marion Stovall. This is Miss Elyse McKenna. We are players at the Ice House Theatre."

I forced myself to open my eyes. Marion was standing beside the constable, a frustrated and upset look on her face. Her gown was completely soaked. In her hand, she was holding one of our stage swords. I cast a glance down at the ice where John—no, Jacob—lay sprawled. The officers were securing his hands with rope.

"That explains why she's dressed in men's clothes. And the man who shoved her in. Who is he?"

"I believe he is Lord John Waldegrave," Marion answered.

"No," I rasped out. My throat burned. "No. He is the pretender."

"Ah," the officer mused loudly. "We've been looking for him. Don't worry, Miss McKenna. We'll get you off the ice and warm in no time. And we'll deal with this piece of rubbish." The officer blew his whistle, calling over some of the other Bow Street Runners to take Jacob into custody.

Marion bent and picked up a bag that had been sitting on the ice. A tuft of dark purple silk stuck out of the bag. It was her Lady MacBeth costume. She'd once told me it was the first role she'd ever played, her first costume, and her very favorite. She always wore the same purple dress whenever she played the part. She'd come back for the costume. To my luck, she'd seen what had happened and, for once, she'd done the right thing. She'd saved me.

"Marion," I whispered.

She shook her head. "Rest, Elyse," she said then smiled softly at me, a million honest apologies in her expression.

"The Hawkings' Workshop," I whispered up to the man who carried me.

"Hawkings' Workshop?" the man asked, looking to his commanding officer.

"Just off the Thames. There," Marion said, pointing. "Miss McKenna has friends there."

The commanding officer nodded, "Very good. Take her there. Quick about it now. And you, Miss Stovall, I need you to come with me."

"Very well," Marion replied.

She set her hand on my shoulder for just a moment.

"Marion…" I whispered.

"I owed you. I'm sorry for what happened," she said with a soft smile then turned and left with the Bow Street Runners.

I closed my eyes.

Hands moved me from person to person, and soon, I was on horseback.

I could feel the rocking movement as the horse trotted across the cobblestones. Someone held me tight against them.

Then, I heard voices.

I heard the Hawkings' footman. Then I heard Isabelle and Master Hawking.

The last voice I heard was Kai's.

"I've got her," Kai said. I felt Kai hold me, carrying me. "I love you, Elyse. Rest and get well. I love you."

Those sweet words rocked me to sleep.

MELANIE KARSAK

THAT NIGHT, I HAD A vivid dream. In my dream, the icy Thames had broken up and the river began to flow once more.

Two ships sailed away from London, their sails illuminated by moonlight.

Standing at the prow of one of the ships was a handsome couple. The man had flowing blond hair. He was joined by a beautiful dark-haired woman. They wore elaborate clothes that were silver and white and trimmed with fine furs and jewels. On their heads, they wore crowns of ice. At the stern stood a boy with dark hair and twinkling eyes. He waved goodbye.

The ships slipped down the Thames, gliding over the dark waves which glimmered with sparkling silver moonlight. They floated downriver until the ships met the moon's reflection. There, the vessels were swallowed by the moon. The fair-haired man and his dark-haired beauty disappeared into the other realm.

32
EPILOGUE

KAI AND I STOOD ON the dock watching the final boxes being loaded onto the ship.

Dressed in a pale yellow gown covered in a blue coat, her hair pulled into a long brown braid, Isabelle rushed down the plank of the ship toward us. She smiled happily.

"We are nearly ready. I've never been at sea before. Papa tells me I will adore it. But I will miss you both," she said happily.

"I have a small gift for you. For luck," I said, handing her an item wrapped in a scarf.

Isabelle opened the gift at once.

I smiled as her face lit up when she saw the small hand mirror.

"This workmanship," she said, touching the elaborate silver filigree.

"I've never seen anything like it!"

"It's quite magical. I'm told that if you look into this mirror under the light of the moon, it will show you your heart's desire."

Isabelle looked up at me, her curious eyes wide. "You jest, I know, but what a fascinating idea. Elyse, I cannot accept this. It's too—"

"I don't need it anymore. I have my heart's desire," I said, beaming up at Kai who was doing his best to look serious. He was failing miserably.

"Safe travels, Miss Hawking," Kai told her.

"Isabelle! We're ready," Master Hawking called from the ship. He turned and waved farewell to us.

"Time to go," she said, clutching the mirror to her chest. "I promise to keep your magic mirror with me at all times," she said with a light laugh then she turned to Kai. "Doctor Murray," she said with a curtsey. "Missus Murray," she added, curtseying to me.

Still getting used to the title, my cheeks burned.

Isabelle ran back aboard the ship.

Kai and I waited, pausing to wave farewell once more, then we headed to our waiting carriage.

"Please take us to the Red Slipper Ballet Academy," Kai told the driver as he helped me climb inside.

The man nodded.

Slipping in beside me, and safely out of sight of prying eyes, Kai slipped his arm around me and pulled me close.

"What is it?" I asked, sensing his discomfort.

"Nothing. I don't like to be near the Thames, that's all."

"Near is one thing. On, or under, is quite something else."

"Quite."

I smiled then stuck my hand out of the window of the carriage. "But today is a warm spring day."

"Yes, Missus Murray, it is. And a fine day for ballet. What time will the Waldegraves be by to inspect the academy?"

"Three. They won't be longer than an hour. Lord Waldegrave just wanted to see the finished studio. Marve and Lizzie will be there for the tour as well."

"Very well. I read in the morning paper that more shooting stars are expected tonight."

"A picnic on the roof then?"

"Shall we make wishes?"

"Of course. But what will you wish for?"

Kai thought deeply then said, "That the Thames never freezes again. And you?"

I reached out and touched his cheek. "Like I told Isabelle, I have all I could have wished for. The course of true love never did run smooth, yet, at last, here we are."

"And here we shall always be," he said, setting a soft kiss on my cheek.

I smiled then looked out the carriage window as we made the final turn away from the Thames. A soft, sweet breeze whisked across the river, carrying with it the scent of new leaves and spring flowers. I stared out at the water. The wave caps shimmered with golden light as if a thousand faeries danced amongst the sprays. I closed my eyes and breathed in the perfume of spring, felt the warmth of Kai's body beside me, and felt the steady beat of my happy heart.

ACKNOWLEDGMENTS

With many thanks to Becky Stephens, Naomi Clewett,

Carrie L. Wells, Jessica Nelson, Tarah Scott,

the Blazing Indie Collective, and my beloved family.

ABOUT THE AUTHOR

Melanie Karsak is the NY Times bestselling author of *The Airship Racing Chronicles, The Harvesting Series,* and *The Celtic Blood Series.* A steampunk connoisseur, zombie whisperer, and heir to the iron throne, the author currently lives in Florida with her husband and two children. She is an Instructor of English at Eastern Florida State College.

Keep in touch with the author online.

www.melaniekarsak.com
www.facebook.com/AuthorMelanieKarsak
ww.twitter.com/melaniekarsak
www.pinterest.com/melaniekarsak

FIND MY BOOKS ON AMAZON.COM

Made in the USA
Middletown, DE
23 June 2019